Enjoy all of these American Girl Mysteries™:

THE SILENT STRANGER

A *Kaya* Mystery by Janet Shaw

THE CURSE OF RAVENSCOURT

A *Samantha* Mystery by Sarah Masters Buckey

DANGER AT THE ZOO

A *Kit* Mystery by Kathleen Ernst

A SPY ON THE HOME FRONT

A *Molly* Mystery by Alison Hart

— A *Samantha* MYSTERY —

THE CURSE OF RAVENSCOURT

by Sarah Masters Buckey

★ American Girl™

Visit our Web site at **americangirl.com**

Printed in China.
05 06 07 08 09 10 LEO 12 11 10 9 8 7 6 5

PICTURE CREDITS
The following individuals and organizations have generously given
permission to reprint illustrations contained in "Looking Back":
pp. 174–175—Notre Dame gargoyles, © Paul Almasy/Corbis;
The Dakota Building, © Monika Smith, Cordaiy Photo
Library Ltd./Corbis; pp. 176–177—spirit body, North Wind
Picture Archives; book, The Manhattan Rare Book Company;
Sherlock Holmes silhouette, © H. Armstrong Roberts/Corbis;
the Fox sisters: Kate Fox and Maggie Fox, Spirit Mediums
from Rochester, New York. Engraved: Kate and Maggie Fox,
Rochester Mediums, T. M. Easterly, Daguerrean. Daguerreotype by
Thomas M. Easterly, 1852. Easterly 172. Missouri Historical Society
Photographs and Prints Collection. Photograph and scan
© 1994–2001, Missouri Historical Society; pp. 178–179—séance,
© Bettmann/Corbis; ghost show, Library of Congress; elevator
sketch, © Bettmann/Corbis; pp. 180–181—elevator operators,
© Hulton-Deutsch Collection/Corbis; The Dakota Building,
© Monika Smith, Cordaiy Photo Library Ltd./Corbis; elevator
panel, photo by Teri Witkowski.

Illustrations by Jean-Paul Tibbles

Library of Congress Cataloging-in-Publication Data

Buckey, Sarah Masters, 1955–
The curse of Ravenscroft : a Samantha mystery / by Sarah Masters Buckey ;
[illustrations by Jean-Paul Tibbles].
p. cm. — "American Girl"
Includes historical information about New York City and its culture in the early
20th century. Summary: When her family temporarily moves into a luxury
apartment building in 1904 Manhattan, eleven-year-old Samantha tries to discover whether a series of mishaps is related to a curse on the building's owner.
ISBN 1-58485-987-3 (pbk.) — ISBN 1-58485-995-4
[1. Apartment houses—Fiction. 2. New York (N.Y.)—History—1898–1951—
Fiction. 3. Mystery and detective stories.] I. Tibbles, Jean-Paul, ill. II. Title.
PZ7.B87983Cu 2005   [Fic]—dc22   2004060241

For J.J.

TABLE OF CONTENTS

1

FEAR AT FIRST SIGHT

Eleven-year-old Samantha Parkington sighed as she looked down the darkened second-floor hall. She had checked all the bedrooms. There was no sign of Jenny.

From the attic came the thud of hammers and the grating screech of saws. Samantha felt a tap on her shoulder. She jumped slightly, then turned and saw Nellie.

"Jenny's not in the library," Nellie reported, frowning.

"Let's try the parlor," suggested Samantha.

The girls hurried down the winding staircase to the first floor. Both were wearing new navy blue winter coats that were identical except for the collars. Samantha's coat had a red velvet collar that went well with her pink cheeks and dark brown hair and eyes. Nellie's coat had a green velvet collar that set off her light brown hair and blue eyes.

Samantha held Jenny's coat in her arms. It was similar to the older girls' coats but smaller, and with a warm, plaid-lined hood instead of a collar.

"Jenny knew she was supposed to get ready," said Nellie, who was carrying Jenny's mittens. "Where can she be?"

As Samantha and Nellie entered the parlor, Samantha called out, "Jenny! Are you in here?"

There was no answer. Samantha looked around the large room. Usually, this cheerful parlor was one of her favorite places in the house. Its plump sofas were soft and welcoming, and its wide windows let the sun stream in. After school, Samantha and her adopted sisters, Nellie, Bridget, and Jenny, liked to sit here and have tea with Aunt Cornelia. They would snack on dainty sandwiches and cakes while they talked and laughed together.

Today, however, the parlor smelled of

wet plaster from the construction upstairs. All the furniture was covered with canvas cloths to keep out dust. The windows were covered, too, so the room had a dark, deserted look.

Samantha peered into the dim corners. "Jenny?" she called again. "If you're hiding, please come out. We have to leave."

Jenny's tear-stained face appeared from behind an armchair. "Don't go without me!"

Samantha walked over to the armchair. "We'd never leave without you," she reassured Jenny. "We've been looking for you. Uncle Gard, Aunt Cornelia, and Bridget are all waiting in the motorcar."

"Can't we stay here?" pleaded seven-year-old Jenny, her lower lip trembling.

"No," said Nellie gently. "Remember how Uncle Gard told us that we're going to go live at Ravenscourt for a few weeks? All the noise here is giving Aunt Cornelia headaches. When the builders are finished, we'll move back in."

Jenny dived back behind the armchair. She

3

emerged clutching her favorite china doll, Louisa-Jane. The doll wore a slightly tattered flowered dress, and had eyes as blue as Jenny's own. "Can Louisa-Jane come with me?"

"Of course," said Samantha. "We wouldn't leave her behind, either." She held out Jenny's coat. "It's cold outside. You'd better bundle up."

Jenny silently pulled on her coat and took the mittens Nellie handed her. Then she walked out into the hall, her head hung low, her small shoulders hunched protectively around Louisa-Jane.

"She seems so upset," Samantha whispered to Nellie as they followed Jenny into the foyer. "Is there anything I can do?"

"No, she'll be all right. It's just that..." Nellie paused and looked around the foyer sadly. "We've been so happy here. It's hard to leave."

We're not really leaving, thought Samantha, feeling puzzled by Nellie's words. *We're only going away for a few weeks. Uncle Gard said it will be more like a vacation than a move.*

Samantha knew what it was like to move from one house to another. Her parents had died when she was little, and she had lived most of her life with her grandmother in the small town of Mount Bedford, New York. That's where she'd first met Nellie O'Malley. The two girls had become best friends—even though Samantha had lived in Grandmary's fancy house and Nellie had worked as a servant girl next door.

A year and a half ago, Uncle Gard and Aunt Cornelia had gotten married, and they had invited Samantha to come live with them in New York City. Soon after Samantha joined her aunt and uncle, she'd heard that Nellie's parents had died. Through some detective work, Samantha had discovered that Nellie and her younger sisters, Bridget and Jenny, were living in a terrible orphanage. Samantha had helped to rescue them from the orphanage and brought them home to her aunt and uncle's house across the street from New York's Gramercy Park.

Samantha had been thrilled when Aunt Cornelia and Uncle Gard had decided to adopt the O'Malley girls. Ever since then, Samantha had thought her life was just about perfect. At last she had the family she had always dreamed about—complete with three sisters.

But with four children, the family's elegant home had begun to seem a little cramped. Aunt Cornelia and Uncle Gard had decided to ease the crowding by building more rooms in the attic. Once the construction was finished, there would be two new bedrooms for the four girls to share—and their very own bathroom.

"We'll only be at Ravenscourt for a few weeks," Samantha said, trying to cheer up Nellie. "And Aunt Cornelia says it's very nice."

Nellie nodded but said nothing. She opened the heavy front door and waited for Jenny to go through first.

"I've always thought it would be great fun to live in an apartment," Samantha continued enthusiastically as she and Nellie followed Jenny out the door. "I'll bet Jenny will like it there."

A cold wind was whipping down the street. "I hope you're right, Samantha," said Nellie as she pushed the carved wooden door closed behind them. "But Bridget and Jenny and I have lived in apartments before."

Before Samantha could reply, Uncle Gard sounded the horn of his Pierce-Arrow motorcar. "Hop in, girls!" he called out. "We'll turn into icicles if we wait out here much longer."

Eight-year-old Bridget was already sitting in the back of the motorcar. Her honey-brown curls were all but hidden under her plaid hood, and she held her teddy bear, Fred, tightly on her lap. Nellie climbed in next to Bridget, Jenny followed her, and Samantha squeezed in last. Samantha shivered as she settled against the leather seat. A wide tonneau cover stretched across the top of the Pierce-Arrow, but the November wind still whistled through the motorcar's open sides.

"Put these over yourselves, girls," said Aunt Cornelia. Reaching back from the front seat, she passed heavy woolen lap robes to the girls while Uncle Gard got out and cranked the car's starter. The cold engine sputtered, then grumbled to life. Uncle Gard jumped back into the driver's seat. "We're off!" he announced.

They drove the car from the quiet of Gramercy Park through the bustle of midtown Manhattan, with its brightly lit stores and busy sidewalks. The streets were teeming with traffic, and Uncle Gard often had to honk and swerve to avoid horse-drawn carriages, bicycles, and other motorcars.

Samantha leaned forward and watched the newspaper boys shouting headlines on the street corners, businessmen hurrying by in tall hats, and women carrying babies in their arms while other children clung to their long skirts.

Sidewalk vendors were roasting chestnuts and smoked sausages. As Samantha smelled the food, she began to feel hungry. She remembered how Aunt Cornelia had said they would eat dinner at Ravenscourt. The building was one of the new "apartment-hotels," where each apartment came fully furnished and staffed with a cook and a maid. Only grumpy Gertrude, the family's housekeeper, would be staying at Ravenscourt with them; their cook, Mrs. Bailey, and their maids, Sally and Martha, were remaining home to take care of the house during construction.

I'll miss them, Samantha thought wistfully. *It will be odd to have strangers living with us.*

As Uncle Gard drove through the changing New York neighborhoods, Samantha saw a group of tired-looking children trudge out of a factory building. She guessed that they were leaving work. Despite the cold wind, several of the children were barefoot and without either hats or jackets. *I hope they have someplace warm to go home to,* she thought.

Samantha glanced over at Nellie, Bridget, and Jenny, who were sitting silently beside her, huddled in their lap robes. She remembered some of the awful places her adopted sisters had lived in the past. First, the whole O'Malley family had shared one cramped room in a tenement on New York's East Side. Later, after their parents died, Nellie, Bridget, and Jenny had been taken in briefly by their Uncle Mike, but he had soon abandoned them. The sisters had been forced to go to the orphanage, where they'd had too much work—and too little food.

No wonder they're scared, Samantha thought. "This will be a nice place," she whispered to Jenny. Jenny glanced up at her gratefully, but she held tight to Louisa-Jane.

Samantha continued to look out the window as they traveled uptown and then turned onto Central Park West, the wide street that followed the western border of Central Park. Traffic began to thin as they drove alongside the huge city park that was like an island of green in the middle of Manhattan. There were more trees and fewer buildings in this part of the city, and the air smelled clean and crisp.

Uncle Gard drove north, past the stately American Museum of Natural History. Finally, he slowed down in front of two towering stone buildings, both facing Central Park.

Over the entrance to the first building, the words *Enderby Towers* were inscribed in bold, black letters.

The second building stood even taller than its neighbor, and it looked newer. An impressive gated archway led up to its main door. Across the archway, fancy gold-plated letters more than two feet high announced *Ravenscourt*. Uncle Gard pulled into a half-circle drive that led up to the archway. He stopped the motorcar in front of a massive statue of a fierce-looking raven. "Here we are!" he announced.

Samantha stared up at the building. Every floor had carved stone decorations around the windows and balconies. The building was so high, she had to crane her neck to see the roof-top. At each corner of the roof stood a carved black raven with its wings spread wide, as if it would fly away at any moment.

"Jiminy!" Samantha exclaimed under her breath. "I never thought Ravenscourt would be so big!"

A red-haired young man wearing a blue doorman's uniform came out from behind the tall wrought-iron gate. "Good afternoon," he greeted them, closing the gate behind himself. "May I help you?"

Uncle Gard told him that they were the Edwards family. "Welcome to Ravenscourt," the young man said, smiling. He gave his hand to Aunt Cornelia as she stepped out of the motorcar. Then he opened the back door, and Samantha climbed out, followed by the other girls.

Uncle Gard set the car's brake and walked over to the raven statue. "Bridget and Jenny, look here!" he said in mock surprise. "I do believe this bird is as big as you are."

The younger girls hurried to the statue. Aunt Cornelia pulled back the veil on her motoring hat and joined them. Samantha was about to follow, too, when she noticed that Nellie was still staring up at Ravenscourt.

"I didn't expect it to be like this—did you, Nellie?" Samantha asked excitedly.

Nellie turned to face her, and Samantha saw that her friend's blue eyes were wide with fear. Nellie looked as if she'd seen a nightmare come to life.

"Nellie, what's wrong?"

"Nothing," said Nellie, quickly recovering herself. "It's just that I've seen ravens like that before. They always bring bad luck."

2
ABOVE THE TREES

Nellie turned away, as if she did not want to say any more. Just then, the redheaded doorman opened the gate. Uncle Gard and Aunt Cornelia shepherded the younger girls through the stone archway, and Samantha and Nellie followed. At the end of the archway, the young doorman ushered them through a pair of glass doors trimmed in polished brass.

Samantha blinked as she walked into the lobby of Ravenscourt. Cut-glass chandeliers hung from the high ceiling, and their bright lights were reflected in a series of gilt-framed mirrors along the walls. Red velvet chairs and sofas were placed in clusters around the lobby, but no one was sitting in them.

"Where is everyone?" Samantha whispered to Nellie. "It's so quiet!"

Nellie just shook her head.

A tall man with thinning brown hair and a carefully groomed mustache entered the lobby from an office to the left of the main door. He was wearing a black suit with a gold pocket watch displayed against his ample stomach.

The doorman tipped his cap to the man. "The Edwards family has arrived, sir, and—"

"Yes, I know, Martin," the man interrupted briskly. The doorman opened his mouth, and Samantha thought he was about to say something. But then he tipped his cap again and quickly went outside.

The man in the black suit turned to Uncle Gard and Aunt Cornelia. "Welcome to Ravenscourt," he said in a crisp British accent. "I'm Mr. Winthrop, manager of the building." He smiled at Uncle Gard. "I understand you're acquainted with Mr. Raven's lawyer, Mr. Sterling."

15

"Mr. Sterling and I are partners in the same law firm," Uncle Gard acknowledged. "He heard that I was interested in renting an apartment for a short period, and he suggested Ravenscourt. When I visited last week, I was pleased to discover that you had a vacancy."

"Quite so," said Mr. Winthrop. He looked concerned. "Ravenscourt opened only a few months ago. We'd expected to be fully occupied by now, but we've had some rather, ah, unexpected occurrences."

Unexpected occurrences? thought Samantha. *I wonder what he means.*

Mr. Winthrop smiled again. "Still, we're most happy to be able to accommodate your family. Please, step this way and I'll show you to your apartment."

Mr. Winthrop led them through the lobby, his shoes tapping loudly on the polished black-and-white marble floor. As they followed him, Samantha made a game of stepping inside the marble squares—never on the cracks. She didn't really believe the superstition that stepping on cracks could bring bad luck, but it was fun to skip over cracks anyway.

When they reached the center of the lobby, Mr. Winthrop turned into a wide alcove. There was a door labeled *Stairs* on one side of the alcove, and two elevators were on the opposite side. Mr. Winthrop ushered them into an elevator compartment unlike any Samantha had ever seen before. It had a brass handrail at waist level, dark wood paneling, and a wood parquet floor. At the far side of the compartment, a wide mirror hung above a leather sofa. *It's like a little parlor,* she thought.

As Samantha moved to the back of the elevator, Bridget reached for her hand. Jenny clung to Aunt Cornelia's hand and stared at the floor suspiciously, as if it might fall from under her feet at any moment. Nellie stared straight ahead, stone-faced. Samantha suddenly realized that none of the O'Malley sisters had ever been on an elevator before. She gave Bridget's hand a reassuring squeeze.

"Twelfth floor," Mr. Winthrop told the

elevator operator, a small, elderly man. The operator nodded and pulled a lever on the controls. The elevator started to climb.

By the time they reached the twelfth floor, Bridget's hand was damp with sweat. But as they exited the elevator alcove, she whispered to Samantha, "Actually, that wasn't so bad."

They turned onto a corridor with gold patterned wallpaper on the walls and Oriental rugs on the floors. A large bronze plaque announced *12th Floor.*

"Only one other apartment is on this top floor, and that belongs to Mr. Raven himself," Mr. Winthrop intoned. "His apartment is on that side"—he motioned to the left—"while yours is over here." They followed Mr. Winthrop to the end of the corridor. Then they turned into a short hall that led directly to an imposing mahogany door. "After you, sir," said Mr. Winthrop, handing Uncle Gard a shiny key.

Before Uncle Gard could unlock the door, it was opened from the inside by a young woman in a white cap and starched white apron. "This is Mary Crosby," said Mr. Winthrop. "She'll be your maid."

Mary smiled a wide, gap-toothed smile and curtseyed politely. "May I take your coats?" she asked as the Edwards family entered. She had twinkling blue eyes and brown curls that peeked out from beneath her cap.

She looks nice, thought Samantha as she handed Mary her coat. *I bet she won't fuss at us the way Gertrude does.*

Gertrude bustled down the hall, looking even grumpier than usual. She had arrived earlier in the day to ready the rooms. Now she met Aunt Cornelia with a list of concerns. "Ma'am, we don't have enough paper to line the shelves. We need more soap, and . . ."

As Gertrude read off her list of problems, Samantha heard her aunt sigh. Glancing up, she saw that Aunt Cornelia looked pale, and there were dark circles under her eyes.

"Thank you, Gertrude," Uncle Gard interjected. "Let's discuss those things later.

Mrs. Edwards is tired right now, and our trunks will be arriving soon. Perhaps you could direct the men to the proper rooms."

Gertrude nodded with an air of self-importance. "Very good, sir. I'll tell the porters where to put everything."

Mr. Winthrop proceeded to give the family a tour of the apartment. He directed them first to the formal parlor, just off the foyer. It was an impressive room with a large marble fireplace, a grand piano, and sofas and chairs covered in royal blue satin.

"Many of our residents entertain frequently," Mr. Winthrop boasted, "and this room provides the perfect gathering place."

Privately, Samantha thought that the Ravenscourt parlor wasn't nearly as welcoming as their parlor at home. The sofa and chairs looked stiff and uncomfortable, and the room was too big to be cozy. She glanced at Nellie to see what she thought, but Nellie was staring at the floor with a worried expression on her face. *Doesn't she like it here?* Samantha wondered.

"When the weather is more pleasant," Mr. Winthrop continued, "you may enjoy stepping out here." He drew back the satin curtains and showed them a pair of double doors that opened onto a small balcony. Samantha saw Jenny's eyes grow big.

"It's like in Rapunzel," whispered Jenny, who loved fairy tales. Samantha nodded, smiling.

"Now you must see the library," said Mr. Winthrop.

He took them across the hall to a small, wood-paneled room where a few new sets of matching books were carefully arranged on shelves. There were two comfortable chairs for reading, but even after Uncle Gard opened the curtains, the library remained quite dark. "I suppose we'll need the electric lights to read in here," Uncle Gard commented.

"Perhaps so," Mr. Winthrop admitted. He explained that the large rooms on the south side of the hall—the parlor, dining room, and bedrooms for the family—were sunny because their windows faced the street. But the smaller rooms on the north side of the hall—the library, pantry, kitchen, and servants' quarters—were darker because they looked out on the air shaft in the center of the building. "Of course," Mr. Winthrop added, "light is not as important in those rooms, is it?"

Samantha thought that servants might like sunlight as much as anyone else would, but she said nothing.

As they returned to the hall, Mr. Winthrop gestured to the apartment's telephone, an elegant silver desk model that sat on a stand by the library door. "It's the new style that doesn't need to be cranked," he said proudly. "We have the most modern conveniences here!"

Mr. Winthrop opened the door to the dining room, which had a wide fireplace and a table large enough to seat twelve. Next, he pointed out the master bedroom, which had its own small sitting room. Further down the hall, Mr. Winthrop showed them a bathroom and two smaller bedrooms.

ABOVE THE TREES

"Bridget and Jenny, you will share this room," said Aunt Cornelia, gesturing to the first of the smaller bedrooms. "Nellie and Samantha, you girls will have the room at the end."

Samantha peeked in and saw a pretty room with twin beds covered in white brocade bedspreads, a white marble fireplace, and a big window with sheer white curtains. She wanted to explore the room, but Mr. Winthrop was continuing his tour. "That's the service entrance," he said, pointing to the door at the end of the hall. "It leads to the servants' elevators and the back stairway."

Across from Samantha and Nellie's room, a short hall led to the servants' quarters. As Mr. Winthrop hurried them through this area, he pointed out Mary's bedroom—a tiny, window-less room—and a slightly larger room with one window that would be Gertrude's bedroom. Returning to the main hall, Mr. Winthrop showed them the pantry, the servants' eating area, and the kitchen, where Samantha could smell roast beef cooking.

Mr. Winthrop stopped outside the kitchen door and introduced them to Mrs. Calloway, the cook. She was a stout, red-faced woman with a double chin that wagged like a turkey's neck. "I can have dinner ready by seven-thirty if that suits you, ma'am," Mrs. Calloway said, and Aunt Cornelia told her that would be fine.

I hope seven-thirty comes soon, thought Samantha, her stomach starting to grumble.

When they returned to the foyer, Mr. Winthrop gave a slight bow. "If I can be of any further service, please don't hesitate to let me know," he said in his clipped British accent. "We hope you enjoy your stay."

After the door had closed behind Mr. Winthrop, Uncle Gard looked at the girls with a mischievous glint in his eyes. "Now that you've seen the apartment, how would you like a bird's-eye view of all of New York?"

"Oh, yes," said Samantha, and Nellie, Bridget, and Jenny nodded.

"Then I have a surprise for you," Uncle Gard said. "Put on your coats and come with me."

The girls followed Uncle Gard back to the elevator alcove. He opened a door across from the elevators that said *Stairs* and, in smaller letters, *To the rooftop.* He led the way upstairs. At the top, he opened another door, and they all stepped out into the cold November wind.

"Is this really the roof?" asked Bridget, looking around hesitantly.

"Yes," said Uncle Gard, leading them around a large chimney. "It's been made into a garden. There's a wall around the edge, but be careful not to lean out over it. I don't want you to fall off."

Beyond the chimney, Samantha saw that the flat roof was laid out with graveled walkways. Along the walkways there were wooden benches and planters filled with soil. In the center of the roof, a tiled fountain stood empty and silent.

"In the summer, flowers bloom up here," said Uncle Gard, leading them to the far side of the roof. "But even at this time of year, you can enjoy the view."

They gathered beside a huge carved raven that perched on a corner of the roof. The cold afternoon was quickly growing dark, and Samantha could see the lights of the city twinkling like fireflies in the distance.

"It's beautiful up here!" exclaimed Bridget, looking out toward the hills and meadows of Central Park. "We're high above the trees!"

Samantha stood against the rough stone wall and peered down at the street. The people and carriages below looked smaller than she could have imagined. She'd never been up so high before, and she suddenly felt dizzy and sick to her stomach.

"It's beautiful," she agreed. She tried to sound enthusiastic, but she was careful not to look down again.

She was glad when Uncle Gard decided it was too cold to stay outside, and they returned to the apartment. Aunt Cornelia met them in the foyer as they were taking off their coats. She told Bridget and Jenny that their trunk had arrived, and Gertrude was now in their room unpacking it.

"Could you go help her?" Aunt Cornelia asked the younger girls. "And make sure you have all your school clothes and books ready for tomorrow." Then she smiled. "And there's a tray of hot chocolate in there to warm you up."

As Bridget and Jenny hurried down the hall to their room, there was a loud knock at the front door.

"It's probably the movers bringing more trunks," said Uncle Gard.

But when Mary answered the door, Samantha saw a broad-shouldered man in a business suit standing with a young lady in a lavender silk dress and a matching feathered hat. The man had gray hair, a jutting jaw, and sharp eyes that seemed to size up the Edwards family at a glance. In a booming voice, he announced that he was Horace Raven, and he introduced his daughter, Eloise.

"Won't you come into the parlor?" asked Aunt Cornelia after the proper introductions were made.

27

As they entered, Samantha noticed that Mr. Raven walked with a limp. Eloise Raven had a pretty smile, and her silk dress was cut in the latest fashion—very snug at the waist, with a full skirt that ended in flounces at the floor.

"We just wanted to say hello," Mr. Raven said as they settled into the blue satin chairs. "I think you'll be happy here. I don't want to boast, but..." He proceeded to list all the special features of Ravenscourt, from its storage areas in the cellar to its modern elevators and rooftop garden.

"There seem to be several new apartment buildings nearby," Uncle Gard said conversationally. "I noticed Enderby Towers next door."

"Yes, but Ravenscourt is definitely the finest building in the area," declared Mr. Raven, going slightly red in the face. "It's much more luxurious than Enderby's building, and taller, too."

Then Mr. Raven chuckled slightly. "I don't

mind telling you, I planned it that way. I've known Walter Enderby a long time. He was always bragging about what a fine place he had up here. I decided to build right next to him and show him what a real apartment building should look like."

Eloise Raven leaned forward in her chair, and strands of her auburn hair escaped from her broad-brimmed hat. "We're very pleased to have your family at Ravenscourt," she told Uncle Gard. Then she turned to Aunt Cornelia. "I recently graduated from the same school you attended, Mrs. Edwards. I remember when you came back to Miss Penwald's Academy and gave a talk on women's suffrage. You were wonderful!"

Aunt Cornelia said that she hoped Eloise would come for tea someday. "We could talk about Miss Penwald's Academy," she suggested.

Samantha was happy to think they were already getting to know their neighbors—and such nice neighbors, too. She looked over at Nellie. She was surprised to see that her friend was biting her lip and eyeing Mr. Raven nervously. *What can be wrong?* Samantha wondered.

Mr. Raven confided to Aunt Cornelia that he was a widower and Eloise was his only child. "I'm sure Eloise would be glad of the society of a lady like yourself, Mrs. Edwards," he said, looking fondly toward his daughter. "When I travel on business, Eloise often stays here with only Miss Simpson."

"Miss Simpson was my tutor," Eloise explained. "Now she's my companion because Father is so often away."

"I travel quite a bit for business, too," said Uncle Gard. "In fact, I must leave tomorrow for Boston. I'll return in a week."

"Well," Mr. Raven boomed, "don't worry about your family while you're gone. We have doormen on duty round the clock, and my manager, Mr. Winthrop, is always available, too. Rest assured, Mr. Edwards, your wife and children will be safe at Ravenscourt."

Samantha glanced over at Nellie, wondering whether this would reassure her. Nellie, however, looked even more concerned. When the Ravens got up to leave, Uncle Gard and Aunt Cornelia walked them to the door. As soon as she and Nellie were alone, Samantha asked Nellie if something was bothering her.

"Oh, Samantha!" Nellie blurted out. "I know Mr. Raven. He's a terrible man. We never should have come here!"

"Why?" asked Samantha, more confused than ever.

Nellie looked around the parlor, as if afraid someone would overhear. "Let's go to our room," she whispered. "I'll tell you there."

3
CURSED

Samantha followed Nellie back to their bedroom. Apart from a few books that Gertrude had deposited on their bedside tables, none of Samantha's and Nellie's personal belongings had arrived yet. The white bedroom looked very tidy, but it felt chilly, and the large fireplace was unlit. Samantha settled down on one of the twin beds and drew its brocade bedspread around her shoulders. "Tell me what's wrong," she urged Nellie.

For a few minutes, Nellie nervously paced the room. Then she sat down on the bed across from Samantha's. "It happened when I was about seven," Nellie began, "back before I even met you, when Dad and Mam were alive, and we were living off Chrystie Street."

Samantha nodded, remembering how Nellie had told her about the apartment where the O'Malleys' family of five had been squeezed into a single room.

Nellie went on to explain that across the street from where her family had lived, there was a tenement building owned by Mr. Raven. "Everyone said he was the meanest landlord in the city," Nellie recalled. "He didn't care if folks were out of work and their children starving—if they didn't pay their rent, he turned them out onto the street."

One cold afternoon, Nellie said, she and Bridget were playing hopscotch on the sidewalk when they heard terrible crying. It was coming from an old woman who lived in Mr. Raven's building. "Her name was Grandma Kildany and she was no more than this tall," said Nellie, putting her hand up to her own forehead. "But people were scared of her. They said she had the second sight."

"Second sight?" Samantha echoed.

Nellie paused, searching for the right words.

"Grandma Kildany could see things and know things that other people couldn't," she said finally. "Almost like a witch. And her keening that day was the worst thing I've ever heard—like all the sadness of the world pouring out of her."

"Why was she crying?"

Nellie gulped and then explained that the Kildany family was very poor. The only heat in their apartment came from a coal-burning stove, and they had little money for coal. They had a new baby—Grandma Kildany's first grandson—who was born early and very small. The family tried hard to keep the tiny infant warm, but no matter how many blankets they wrapped him in, the baby shivered in the cold apartment. One day, his grandmother found him dead in his cradle.

"How awful!" Samantha gasped.

Nellie nodded. The day after the baby died, she continued, Mr. Raven happened to come knocking at the door, demanding his usual month's rent. When Grandma Kildany saw the landlord, she flew into a fury. She blamed him for her grandson's death and said he'd be cursed till the end of his days. As he backed away from the furious old woman, Mr. Raven tripped and tumbled down the stairs.

"You see how he walks, don't you?" Nellie asked. "He broke his leg that day, and he still limps. People say that was the beginning of the curse."

Samantha felt a shiver of fear and she drew the bedcover more tightly around her shoulders. *Mr. Raven does limp,* she told herself. *But Grandmary always said it was foolish to believe in superstitions.* "Are you sure Mr. Raven is cursed, Nellie?"

Before Nellie could answer, there was a quick knock at the bedroom door, which the girls had left ajar. "Come in," Samantha called out.

Mary bustled into the room, carrying a brass bucket filled with large chunks of coal. She began building a fire in the fireplace. "Beggin' your pardon," she said as she worked. "But I heard you talkin' about the curse on Mr. Raven."

"It's true, isn't it?" asked Nellie.

Mary shook her head sadly. "Surely I've heard the story of the Kildany curse often enough," she said with a soft Irish lilt. "Of course, I can't say it's true, for I don't know that part of town myself. But with everything that's been happenin' since, well . . ."

"What's happened?" Samantha and Nellie asked together.

"I shouldn't be talkin' about it," Mary said, hesitating as she bent down and arranged the coal on the hearth.

Samantha and Nellie insisted that they wanted to know everything. Finally Mary told them that, since Mr. Raven had been cursed, his wife had died in a carriage crash and one of his buildings had burned down. "Now people are sayin' Ravenscourt is cursed. One poor worker died when they was buildin' here. Fell right down the elevator shaft, he did, may he rest in peace." Mary crossed herself and then heaved a sigh. "'Course, Mr. Raven *told* everybody it was an accident, but . . ." Her voice trailed off.

"But accidents *can* happen to anyone, can't they?" said Samantha, trying to convince herself. "Maybe it wasn't the curse at all."

Mary gave her an odd glance. "Yes, miss, you're probably right," she said. Somehow, however, Samantha did not feel reassured.

"And surely, anyone could have a new furnace break down twice in one week, too," said Mary as she straightened up from building the fire. "Ah, well, Mr. Winthrop says it'll be fixed by morning." Mary put a match to the fire, and bright flames shot up. "This'll keep you warm till then."

After Mary left, Nellie sat silently on her bed, her face looking drawn and pinched. "I wish we could leave Ravenscourt this very moment," she confided to Samantha. "You heard what Mary said—it's cursed."

Samantha looked around herself uneasily. When she had first seen the white bedroom, she'd thought it looked pretty. Now the room seemed cold and unfriendly. "Do you think we should talk to Uncle Gard?" Samantha asked.

Nellie shook her head. "He'd think it was silly."

Samantha nodded. She knew Nellie was right. Uncle Gard believed in scientific facts, not superstitions. He'd probably laugh at rumors of a curse.

"If Ravenscourt really is cursed," Samantha said slowly, "then more bad things will happen here, won't they?"

"Yes," Nellie agreed. She clasped her arms tightly around herself and shuddered slightly.

While Nellie stared into the fire, lost in her own thoughts, Samantha stood up and strolled around the room. Trying to seem as casual as she could, she stepped over to the closet and flung open its door. Except for a few hangers, it was empty. Next Samantha crouched down and, pretending to tighten her bootlaces, looked under the twin beds. There wasn't even a dust ball on the floor.

There's nothing in here to be scared of, she told herself, and she sat back down on her bed. Her eyes fell on the Sherlock Holmes book,

The Hound of the Baskervilles, that Gertrude had placed on her bedside table. Samantha had just started reading Sherlock Holmes stories, and the thought of the great detective gave her an idea.

"We could be like detectives and watch and see what happens," she suggested to Nellie. "If we could prove that the building is cursed, Uncle Gard would listen to us."

"I guess so," said Nellie. She looked away from the fire and her eyes searched Samantha's face. "But let's not say anything to Bridget or Jenny. I don't want to worry them, and—"

Just then, the fire popped loudly. Both girls jumped as sparks sprayed onto the hearth.

"And let's be very careful, too," Nellie continued, and she got up and secured the fire screen in front of the fireplace.

"We will be," Samantha promised.

Dinner was served promptly at seven-thirty. A fire blazed in the dining-room fireplace, but the room was still cold. Aunt Cornelia gave each of the girls a warm woolen shawl. "Put these on, and you'll be snug as bugs," she advised as they sat down at the long table.

The dinner began with a creamy tomato soup, followed by a fish course of fried trout with slivered almonds. As Samantha nibbled her last bit of crispy fish, she decided that Mrs. Calloway was almost as good a cook as Mrs. Bailey at home.

Uncle Gard got up during dinner to put more coal on the fire. "Perhaps this building isn't as up-to-date as Mr. Raven promised us," he said as they were finishing their main course of roast beef and gravy with mashed potatoes. He reached for Aunt Cornelia's hand. "Are you sure you and the girls will be all right here while I'm away?"

"Women are traveling round the world these days," Aunt Cornelia said with a laugh. "I'm sure the girls and I can spend a night without central heating—especially since we have these lovely fireplaces."

As Mary brought in generous slices of cinnamon-scented apple pie, everyone heard the popping sound of the radiators coming to life. "Well, the boiler must be working again," Uncle Gard said, looking relieved. "I guess we're all tired. Let's enjoy dessert and get a good night's sleep."

❧

Samantha and Nellie were so tired that they didn't talk much after Aunt Cornelia tucked them into bed. Samantha huddled under her covers and tried not to think about the curse. She was just drifting off to sleep when she heard the click of the door opening. Bridget tiptoed into the room and over to her sister's bed. "Nellie!" she whispered. "Are you awake?"

"Now I am," Nellie said groggily. "What's wrong?"

"It's Jenny," Bridget said urgently. "She's crying, and she wants you."

"All right," Nellie whispered back. "But let's be quiet so we don't wake up Samantha."

Samantha listened to them tiptoe out. She

heard the muffled sounds of sobs coming from the next room. *Maybe I can help comfort Jenny, too,* she thought. *She loves to hear fairy tales.*

Samantha eased out from under her covers, pulled on her robe, and slipped down the hall to Bridget and Jenny's room. As she was about to open the door, she heard Jenny say, "Sing it just the way Mam used to, Nellie."

Then she heard Nellie softly begin an Irish melody. Samantha paused. She remembered that sometimes, when the younger girls were very upset, all they wanted to hear were Nellie's stories of their parents and the lullabies their mother used to sing.

They've been sisters all their lives, but I've only been their sister less than a year, Samantha told herself. *Maybe they want to be alone together.* With a heavy heart, she went back to her room and tried to get warm under the covers. Sleep was just stealing over her again when she heard a soft scrabbling behind her head.

She bolted upright, her heart pounding. Thoughts raced through her head . . . the curse

on Mr. Raven ... the worker who had died
in the elevator shaft. Could someone—or
something—be inside the walls, struggling
to get out?

4
A WARNING

Samantha sat still in the darkness, listening. Then she heard it again—a soft scrabbling that sounded like fingers grasping for a hold. A shiver ran down her back. She felt as if long cold hands were reaching out to grab her from behind.

She vaulted out of bed and headed for the door. Then she paused, her hand on the doorknob. She wanted to join Nellie in Bridget and Jenny's room. But what if the younger girls had finally fallen asleep? She could knock on Aunt Cornelia and Uncle Gard's door. But she didn't want to disturb them, either.

As she stood wondering what to do, Samantha heard the scrabbling again. Now it sounded farther away—as if it were coming from the ceiling near the fireplace. She gathered her courage and switched on the light. For a moment, the sound stopped. Samantha held her breath, hoping that, whatever it was, it had gone away.

Then she heard it again. But now that the room was lit, the soft noise didn't sound nearly as frightening as it had in the dark. It reminded Samantha of the time a squirrel had gnawed its way into the attic of Grandmary's house in Mount Bedford.

A squirrel! Samantha thought with relief. *That's what it must be.*

Comforted by this thought, Samantha kept the light on but returned to bed. *I'll just lie here and wait for Nellie,* she thought.

❧

The next thing she knew, it was morning. It was raining outside, but light filtered through the white curtains. Nellie's bed was still empty, and Samantha guessed she'd spent the whole night in Bridget and Jenny's room. Samantha quickly dressed in her school clothes and followed the smell of bacon and coffee to the dining room. There she found Aunt Cornelia and Uncle Gard at the table. Uncle Gard was wearing a business suit and was finishing his last bit of poached eggs. Aunt Cornelia was still in her dressing gown, and she had not yet eaten her eggs and bacon. She looked as if she hadn't slept well.

When Uncle Gard saw Samantha, he smiled. "You're up bright and early, Sam! I was just about to leave to catch my train." He pushed away his plate. "Want to come down to the lobby and see me off?"

After Uncle Gard kissed Aunt Cornelia good-bye, he and Samantha walked together toward the elevators. When the first elevator arrived, they were the only passengers, and the elevator operator looked half-asleep. "I'm glad to have a chance to talk with you this morning, Sam," said Uncle Gard as the elevator doors closed. He looked so serious that Samantha wondered if she had done something wrong.

"It's about Aunt Cornelia," Uncle Gard continued in a low tone. "She's been rather tired lately. We must help her get more rest. If you and the other girls have little problems while I'm gone this week, try to solve them yourselves. Try not to trouble your aunt, all right?"

Have we been bothering Aunt Cornelia too much? Samantha worried. "We'll be on our best behavior," she promised Uncle Gard. "We won't trouble her at all."

"Good girl!" Uncle Gard said, patting her on the shoulder. "I knew I could count on you."

It was still raining hard outside, so Uncle Gard hugged Samantha in the lobby, and then she waved good-bye to him from behind the lobby's glass doors. When Samantha turned to go back upstairs, she noticed that Martin, the redheaded doorman, was on duty again in the lobby. He stepped forward.

"Let me get the elevator for you," he offered. His jacket was damp from the rain and his hair was tousled. As he pushed the button, Samantha noticed a red mark like a slash across the back of his right hand.

"Did you hurt yourself?" she asked.

"Oh, no," Martin said, quickly putting his hand in his pocket. "It's only a little cut." While they waited for the elevator, Martin asked how Samantha and her family liked Ravenscourt so far.

"It's very nice," she said politely.

"No problems, I hope?" Martin inquired.

Samantha hesitated. "Well, the heat wasn't working last night," she told him. "And then there was the squirrel."

"Squirrel?" Martin looked confused. "In the building?"

"Yes, last night—" Samantha began, but just then the elevator's cage-like doors opened and Mr. Winthrop stepped out. He looked immaculate in a carefully pressed black suit, starched shirt, and white gloves. He drew out his pocket watch and glanced at it significantly.

"Mr. Ayresworth is waiting for his taxi,"

A Warning

Mr. Winthrop said in his dignified English accent. "Please see to it, Martin."

Samantha got into the elevator and asked the operator for the twelfth floor. She enjoyed the giddy feeling of soaring upward. *I like being up high,* she decided. *As long as I don't have to look down.*

Smiling, Samantha stepped off the elevator. As the elevator's doors closed behind her, she turned and saw the brass plaque. Over the engraved *12th Floor,* a huge *13* was now scrawled in red. It looked as if blood were dripping down the shiny brass.

"Oh!" Samantha exclaimed. She felt her stomach coil with fear.

She wanted to run to Aunt Cornelia, but she remembered her promise to Uncle Gard. *Maybe I can clean it up myself,* Samantha thought reluctantly. She took out her handkerchief and dabbed cautiously at the plaque. She was relieved to find that the red liquid looked and smelled like paint, not blood.

Samantha reached up to wipe off a little

more. The liquid was sticky, and it smeared her handkerchief.

"What are you doing?" a young woman's voice demanded. Samantha turned and saw Eloise Raven. She was dressed in a dark green coat and hat, and she had a small brown and white terrier on a leash. The dog yipped excitedly at Samantha.

Samantha explained that she was trying to clean up the sign. Miss Raven strode up to the plaque and stared at it for a moment. Then she took a deep breath and asked, "How long has this been here?"

"Uncle Gard and I didn't see it when we walked to the elevator a little while ago," Samantha said.

"So someone just did it," Miss Raven concluded. "Wait here. I'll take Juno home and get some things from my art supplies." Miss Raven disappeared into her apartment. She returned without the dog, but with several rags and a jar of strong-smelling paint remover.

"Who would do something like this?"

A WARNING

Samantha wondered aloud as she helped Miss Raven dampen the rags with paint remover.

"Someone who wants to hurt my father!" Miss Raven exclaimed angrily. She took a rag and rubbed at the red paint. "But they're not going to get away with it this time."

"Miss Raven?" Samantha asked hesitantly. "Have there been other . . ."—she tried to think of the right word—"um, other things happening in the building?"

Miss Raven nodded. "You may call me Eloise," she directed. "And yes, there have been some other incidents."

Samantha wondered what the other "incidents" were, but she was afraid to ask. She kept scrubbing at the paint, and in a few minutes she and Eloise had wiped the brass plaque clean. Eloise gathered up the stained rags and then turned to Samantha. "If you see other mean tricks like this, would you tell me?"

"Yes," Samantha agreed, wondering what other mean tricks she might discover.

"I'd appreciate, though, if you wouldn't mention what you saw here to the residents of other apartments," Eloise added. "There are enough rumors going around already."

A mean trick, that's all it was, Samantha told herself as she walked back to her apartment. Then it occurred to her that Ravenscourt didn't include the ground floor in its numbering system. The floor above the lobby was numbered *One,* the floor above that *Two,* and so on. *If the ground floor were counted, this would be the thirteenth floor,* she realized.

Samantha had often heard that the number thirteen was unlucky. Now worry filled her stomach like a lump of ice swallowed whole. *Are we really living on the thirteenth floor of a cursed building?* she wondered as she entered her apartment.

Inside, Samantha found that Nellie, Bridget, and Jenny were all dressed and ready for school. Cornelia, still in her dressing gown, smiled and said she hoped they would have a good day. Gertrude sourly told the girls to hurry up, as she was going to escort them to school.

On the way down to the lobby, Nellie, Bridget, and Jenny giggled as the elevator stopped at various floors to pick up passengers. "This is fun!" Bridget whispered as the elevator started again after picking up a man on the fourth floor.

Gertrude, however, shook her head dolefully. "You can't trust these modern inventions!" she muttered under her breath. She clutched the handrail until the elevator lurched to a halt on the main floor.

When they reached the lobby doors, Martin held an umbrella over their heads and walked them to a tall, black horse-drawn carriage. Since Ravenscourt was far from the girls' schools, Uncle Gard had arranged for the hired carriage to drive them every day. Samantha's school was closest, and the driver would drop her off first. He would stop at Bridget and Jenny's school next, and then take Nellie to her school. In the afternoon, the order would be reversed.

On this chilly morning, the taxi driver steered his horses carefully through the busy traffic as rain lashed at the roof of the carriage. The streets were so crowded that it took almost an hour for the carriage to reach Samantha's school.

"Mind you look for the carriage at the end of the day!" Gertrude said curtly as Samantha stepped down from the passenger compartment.

"Good-bye!" called Nellie, Bridget, and Jenny.

The school day passed slowly for Samantha. When she tried to do her multiplication problems, all she could think about was the dripping red *13.* And when the class was reading *The Legend of Sleepy Hollow,* Samantha shivered as she read, "Certain it is, the place still continues under the sway of some witching power."

Can a place really be cursed? she wondered.

By the end of the day, the rain had stopped but the sky was still gray. While other children hurried home, Samantha waited anxiously in the schoolyard for the hired carriage. When it finally arrived, only Nellie was sitting inside it.

"Where are the others?" Samantha asked as she climbed in.

With a solemn face, Nellie told her that they'd gone to drop off Bridget and Jenny in the morning, but the doors to the younger girls' school had been locked. A sign outside the school had announced that there was an outbreak of chicken pox among the students. By order of the health officials, the school had been temporarily closed until further notice.

"The first thing Gertrude wanted to know was whether my sisters and I had already had chicken pox," Nellie said. "I know I had it when I was little—Mam told me I called it 'chicken box.' But I don't know about Bridget and Jenny. I'm not sure they were even born then."

"I had it when I was six years old," Samantha recalled. "I remember Grandmary giving me rice pudding because there were pox inside my throat and I couldn't eat anything else."

"Oh, Samantha, what if Bridget and Jenny catch chicken pox?" said Nellie. She nervously twisted her handkerchief in her hands. "What if we're all under the Ravenscourt curse?"

Samantha remembered how Nellie's parents had both died of the flu. She tried to comfort her friend. "Don't worry," she said kindly. "Bridget and Jenny aren't sick yet, are they?"

"No," said Nellie. "They seemed fine this morning."

"And even if they do catch chicken pox, they'll surely get better soon," Samantha reassured her. "You and I had it, and we're fine."

"Maybe you're right," said Nellie. She looked out the carriage window and watched the city traffic pass by. "I only hope nothing else happens at Ravenscourt."

Samantha bit her lip. Nellie, noticing her silence, turned back to her. "Something else *has* happened, hasn't it?"

Reluctantly, Samantha told her about the number thirteen on the sign. "When Eloise and I wiped it off, it was paint—not blood or anything like that," Samantha concluded. "Eloise said someone was just playing a mean trick."

"Who would want to do that?" Nellie

asked. "And how would they do it? It would be hard for someone to sneak inside the building. The doormen would stop anyone they didn't know."

"That's true," said Samantha, and then she had a terrible thought. "What if it's someone who lives in the building? Or works there?"

For a few minutes the girls rode along in silence. Samantha stared down at her hands. There was red paint under one of her nails, left from when she had cleaned the sign. She remembered the slash of red on Martin's hand that morning, and she told Nellie about it. "He said it was a cut," Samantha added. "But it could have been paint. Do you think he could be the one who's trying to scare us?"

"He *seems* nice," Nellie said hesitantly.

"Yes," Samantha agreed. "But if we're going to be detectives, we should keep an eye on him. We should watch anyone at Ravenscourt who acts suspiciously."

"What if the '13' wasn't painted by a person?" asked Nellie as the carriage pulled up in front of Ravenscourt. "What if the building really is cursed?"

Samantha looked up at the massive building. Outlined against the gray sky, the carved ravens stared down at her from the rooftop. "It can't be cursed," she told Nellie, trying to sound brave. But inside, she felt a shiver of fear.

5

SUDDEN DEPARTURE

As Samantha and Nellie dressed for school the next morning, they could hear laughter coming from Bridget and Jenny's room. Samantha was glad the younger girls weren't sick, but she felt a little envious that they could stay home from school. *I wish I could play all day today!* she thought as she buttoned up her high boots.

When Samantha and Nellie were ready to leave, Gertrude told them they would be allowed to travel in the hired carriage by themselves. "You are both big girls," she said. "I know you can be trusted."

Privately, Samantha wondered whether Gertrude really trusted them—or if the housekeeper just wanted to avoid the elevator. Either way, though, she and Nellie were happy to be on their own. They were swinging their arms cheerfully as they walked down the hall together—until they reached the brass sign by the elevator.

Samantha looked at Nellie. Yesterday afternoon, Nellie had avoided even glancing at the plaque, as if she were afraid that the curse might somehow rub off on her. Now Nellie was studying it, but she was careful to keep about five feet away.

Samantha walked up to the plaque. It still smelled of paint remover. "It seems all right now," she said. "There are just a few traces of paint left, here on the side. Eloise and I must have missed them."

Nellie gestured at the wood floor under the plaque. "Was there paint on the floor yesterday?"

"No, at least none that I saw." Samantha looked down. "I don't see any now, either."

"Neither do I," Nellie said slowly. "But if somebody stood here and painted a big red

'13' on the sign, don't you think some paint would have dripped, especially if the person was working fast?"

Samantha ran her hand over the smooth brass. It was hard and shiny—not the kind of surface that would easily absorb paint. "I guess you're right. It probably would've dripped."

"But it didn't," said Nellie, looking around anxiously. She took a step backward. "Samantha, this must be a sign of the curse. Thirteen always means bad luck."

Samantha moved away from the plaque, too. She jumped when she heard the elevator doors open just a few feet away.

The redheaded doorman, Martin, stepped off the elevator carrying a package wrapped in brown paper. He seemed surprised to see the girls, but he tipped his cap and said good morning. Then he headed down the hall toward the Ravens' apartment. He turned the corner. The girls heard him knock on the door and call out, "Delivery for Miss Raven!"

Samantha and Nellie looked at each other.

"Remember the red mark on his hand yesterday?" Samantha whispered.

Nellie nodded. Then, as if they could read
each other's thoughts, both girls ran down the
corridor. They ducked into the short hall that
led to their apartment, hiding behind the
corner so Martin wouldn't see them.

A moment later, they heard a door close
and footsteps coming down the wide corridor.
Suddenly the footsteps came to a halt.

"What do you think he's doing?" Nellie
whispered.

Samantha felt her heart pounding. "I don't
know."

Ever so carefully, the girls ventured to
look around the corner. Samantha saw Martin
standing halfway down the corridor. His back
was to them, and he was examining the brass
plaque.

Samantha quickly ducked back behind the
corner. Nellie drew back in, too. They heard
more footsteps, and then the sound of an
elevator arriving. Martin said something to

the operator. Only after they heard the elevator doors close again did the girls venture out from their hiding place.

"Did you see how he was looking at the sign?" Samantha asked Nellie as they walked back toward the elevator alcove. "He must know about the '13'—but how?"

"Maybe Miss Raven told him about it," Nellie suggested.

"Maybe," Samantha agreed. Her heart was still thudding in her chest. "But she asked me to keep it a secret. Why would she tell the doorman?" Samantha shook her head. "Something strange is going on."

She paused, took a deep breath, and then stepped up to examine the plaque more closely. "Look," she said to Nellie, who still stayed several feet away. "It's hanging from hooks— like a picture. Someone could have taken it off the wall and painted it, then put it up again later. That would explain why there's no paint on the floor here."

Nellie bit her lip. "I guess so," she agreed.

"But whoever painted it must have been right here in the building yesterday morning," Samantha continued. She and Nellie looked at each other. One name was on their minds: Martin.

"We don't know anything for sure," Nellie reminded her.

"Yes," Samantha agreed. "But seeing Martin here could be our first real clue. We know he was in the building yesterday—I saw him in the lobby. And he had the red mark on his hand."

Samantha pressed the *Down* button by the elevators, and when the first car arrived, they took it to the ground floor. Martin had returned to the lobby, and Samantha noticed that he was tall—over six feet—and looked athletic. She guessed that he easily could have carried the large brass plaque. She tried to see whether there was still a red mark on his right hand, but this morning he was wearing white gloves.

It was drizzling outside, and Martin again held an umbrella for the girls as he helped them into their carriage. "Have a good day at school!" he said, smiling. Samantha felt suddenly ashamed of her suspicions. *Martin wouldn't have done such a mean thing,* she told herself. *But if he didn't, who did?*

❧

At school, Samantha told herself not to think about the mysterious events at Ravenscourt. *There's no such thing as the curse of Ravenscourt— and no other bad things will happen,* she tried to convince herself.

When she and Nellie returned to the apartment, however, Gertrude met them at the door. Her mouth was set in a tight frown. "Bridget and Jenny have both come down with chicken pox," the housekeeper said grimly as she took the girls' coats.

The color drained from Nellie's face. "Oh, no! Can we get a doctor?"

Aunt Cornelia came into the foyer. "Dr. Brickfield was here a few hours ago, Nellie dear," she reassured her. "He said we shouldn't be too concerned—chicken pox is usually not a serious illness in children." Samantha thought she saw a flicker of worry pass over Aunt Cornelia's face, but a moment later it was gone.

"What they need most is rest, and they're in their beds right now," Aunt Cornelia added. She smiled at Nellie and Samantha. "Since you girls have already had chicken pox, you may go visit them."

Samantha and Nellie hurried to the younger girls' room. Samantha saw that Bridget had red blotchy spots scattered over her face, and her brown curls lay in damp ringlets. Jenny had only a few spots, but her blue eyes looked dull and tired.

"How are you?" Nellie asked anxiously. "Have you been eating at all?"

"Oh, yes," said Bridget, smiling weakly. "Gertrude has been bringing us soups and jellies and puddings—anything we wanted. She's been so nice."

"Gertrude?" Samantha echoed.

"Aye," said Mary, who came into the room carrying two bowls of rice pudding. "She's been fussin' over the girls all day. Says she can't stand to see a sick child suffer."

Samantha shook her head in amazement. It was hard to imagine grumpy old Gertrude being nice. Samantha tried to think of something to entertain the sick girls. "Do you want to play cards?" she asked them.

"Or dominoes?" Nellie offered.

Both the younger girls said they were too tired to play a game. "Will you sing me one of Mam's songs again?" Jenny asked Nellie.

While Nellie began to sing, Samantha slipped out of the younger girls' room. She went to her own room, picked up her copy of *The Hound of the Baskervilles,* and took it down the hall to the library. It was still drizzling outside, and the light that seeped through the library windows looked like gray fog. Samantha switched on the electric lamp and curled up in one of the armchairs with her Sherlock Holmes mystery.

Well, Watson, what do you make of it? Samantha was reading when the telephone jangled just outside the library door. Samantha jumped slightly and waited for someone to answer it.

The telephone rang again. "Mary, answer the 'phone!" Gertrude called out. But Mary didn't come, and Samantha guessed that she hadn't heard Gertrude's summons.

Samantha wondered what she should do. The telephone rarely rang at home, and when it did, one of the servants usually picked it up and said, "Edwards residence!" The 'phone jangled once more, and Samantha decided to answer the way she'd heard Aunt Cornelia do it. She picked up the earpiece and called out "Hello!" into the receiver.

"Great Caesar's ghost, Cornelia!" exclaimed a piercing voice that Samantha recognized as belonging to Mrs. Pitt, Aunt Cornelia's mother. "Why are you still there? You could be in great danger! I told you this morning that you should leave. I was just 'phoning to be sure you'd listened to me."

"I'm sorry, but—" Samantha started to explain.

Mrs. Pitt cut her off. "No excuses, Cornelia. You *must* leave now. Don't worry about the girls. You must look after yourself. If Gard were there, he'd say the same thing—"

"Mrs. Pitt," Samantha broke in, "this is Samantha. I'll go get Aunt Cornelia."

"What?" shouted Mrs. Pitt. "Good heavens, you silly girl, why didn't you say so at once? Yes, get her immediately."

Samantha rushed down the hall to Aunt Cornelia's room and told her that her mother was on the telephone.

"Oh, goodness!" said Aunt Cornelia and hurried to the 'phone. Samantha closed the door that led from the library to the hall. She tried not to listen to Aunt Cornelia's conversation. But the few things she did overhear sounded frightening.

". . . I can't leave the girls," she heard Aunt Cornelia protest.

"And we're not *sure* that . . ."

Then finally she closed with, "Very well, Mother. Yes, I'll 'phone you later."

After Aunt Cornelia hung up, Samantha stayed frozen in her seat. *What could the "great danger" possibly be?* she agonized. *Could the curse be real?*

When Gertrude looked in the library a short while later, Samantha was still rooted in her chair, dazed by what she'd overheard. "Oh, there you are," the housekeeper said gruffly. "Your aunt wishes to see you in her room."

Samantha hoped desperately that Aunt Cornelia might explain the mysterious call. *She'll probably laugh and say it was some sort of misunderstanding,* Samantha told herself.

But as Samantha entered the room, she found that Aunt Cornelia looked pale and unhappy. Even worse, she was wearing her gray traveling suit and her blue fur-trimmed coat. She was sitting by her dressing table, and a small suitcase and her sturdy mahogany umbrella stood on the floor beside her.

"Samantha, dear, I wanted to speak with you because I have to leave tonight," Aunt Cornelia told her. "My mother is ill, and I am going to Connecticut to see her. Gertrude will be in charge while I'm gone."

Samantha was stunned. *Mrs. Pitt didn't sound sick at all,* she thought. But she couldn't tell Aunt Cornelia that she didn't believe her. She tried to think of something to say. "Will you see Agatha, Agnes, and Alice in Connecticut?" she finally asked, referring to Aunt Cornelia's younger sisters, who often came to visit the Edwards family.

Aunt Cornelia seemed taken aback by the question. Then she said quickly, "Why, yes, of course I shall. They'll help me take care of Mother, I'm sure." Aunt Cornelia stood up and walked over to Samantha. "The other girls are resting, and I don't want to disturb them," she said, putting her hand gently on Samantha's shoulder. "Give them my love and tell them I'll 'phone from Connecticut tomorrow to see how they are feeling."

Samantha nodded. "When will you be back?" she ventured.

"I hope to return soon—I'll let Gertrude know the exact day." Aunt Cornelia reached down and gave Samantha a kiss on the cheek. Her face felt damp, as if she had been crying, but she smiled at Samantha. "Good-bye, my dear, and mind Gertrude while I'm gone."

Samantha's heart fell as she watched her beautiful aunt walk quickly down the hall, her suitcase in one hand, her sturdy umbrella in the other. *She must be afraid of something here at Ravenscourt,* Samantha thought, feeling scared and hollow inside. *But why would she leave us?*

Suddenly, Samantha's eyes began to fill with tears, and she felt that she needed to be alone. As she headed down the hall to her bedroom, she passed Bridget and Jenny's room. The door was ajar, and Samantha saw that Nellie was sitting on Bridget's bed and reading both girls a story.

They're awake! Why did Aunt Cornelia say they were resting? Samantha wondered, more confused than ever. For a moment, she stood outside the door. She decided that it wouldn't do to let the younger girls see her upset. She wiped her eyes and forced herself to smile.

"May I come in?" she asked, knocking on the door.

The other girls welcomed her. Trying to sound matter-of-fact, Samantha gave them Aunt Cornelia's message. Bridget and Jenny didn't seem too concerned about Aunt Cornelia's absence. After all, Aunt Cornelia had gone to visit her mother before—though never while Uncle Gard was away.

Nellie's face creased with worry, but she didn't ask any questions. She picked up the book she'd been reading to her sisters. "And the big wolf—" she began.

Then a scream broke the evening quiet.

6

A DANGEROUS JOURNEY

Samantha and Nellie ran toward the kitchen, where the scream seemed to have come from. There they found Mrs. Calloway standing on a chair. She was very red in the face and her double chins were quivering.

"What in heaven's name is the matter?" demanded Gertrude, who rushed into the room a moment later with Mary just behind her.

"A rat!" Mrs. Calloway cried out. "There's a rat in my kitchen!" She shuddered with horror. "When I reached into the cabinet, I almost touched it!"

Samantha breathed a sigh of relief. A rat was certainly unpleasant, but it wasn't nearly as bad as what she'd imagined when she'd heard the scream. She sneaked a look at Nellie, and then both girls had to fight back giggles. The stout Mrs. Calloway looked so silly standing on that chair, as if an army of rats were set to attack her.

Gertrude pursed her lips. "Mary," she ordered, "go downstairs immediately and see the manager, Mr. Winthrop. Inform him of the problem. Tell him we expect a rat catcher here first thing in the morning."

"Yes, ma'am," Mary said, and with her skirt swishing, she hurried off down the hall.

Gertrude helped Mrs. Calloway down from her perch, and then sniffed the air meaningfully. There was a tantalizing smell of roast lamb and onions. "I think you might want to attend to the roast," she told the cook. "We don't want it to burn, do we?"

"But what if the rat comes back?" the large cook quavered. "It might bite me!"

"It will do nothing of the sort," Gertrude said firmly. "We'll have it trapped in no time." Gertrude stopped for a moment. "Oh, great heavens, I should have told Mary to get rat traps, too." She sighed. "Now I suppose I must go downstairs myself."

Gertrude looked pained by this idea. Nellie came to her rescue. "I'll go find Mary," she said, and Samantha offered to go with her.

Together, the two girls hurried to the elevator. When they first reached the lobby, they didn't see Mary. Then Samantha spotted her standing in a far corner with Martin. Their heads were close together, as if they were speaking in confidence. Mary looked startled when she saw the girls. "Oh!" she exclaimed, taking a step back from Martin. "I was just comin' upstairs."

The girls gave Mary the message about the rat traps. Martin raised his eyebrows. "Rats?" he said, sounding surprised. "I haven't seen any sign of rats in the cellar."

"Well, one of 'em found its way to our kitchen," Mary told him. "Cook nearly screamed her head off when she saw it."

Martin offered to go find traps for Mary. Samantha and Nellie headed back to their apartment. As they got off the elevator, however, Samantha remembered her promise to Eloise. "I said I'd let her know if anything else went wrong," she explained to Nellie. "Do you think she'd want to know about the rat?"

"I guess so," Nellie said uncertainly.

Together, the girls knocked at the door of the Ravens' apartment. They heard barking in the distance and a voice saying, "Calm down, Juno!" A thin young maid in a white apron answered the door.

"We'd like to see Miss Raven, please," Samantha told her shyly.

"I'll see if Miss Raven is receiving visitors," the maid said. "Would you care to wait in the parlor?"

The maid ushered them into a large, elaborately decorated room that made Samantha feel very small. The drapes were made of gold velvet, and the sofas and chair cushions were covered in velvet, too. White lace doilies sat delicately on the tables, and every spare surface was filled with framed pictures and china figurines. Everything looked so perfect that both Samantha and Nellie were scared to sit down. They stood waiting nervously in the center of the room until Eloise strode into the parlor. She was wearing a pale green dress with a sweeping train, several strings of pearls around her neck, and dangling pearl earrings.

"Please sit down," she said, smiling. "I was just getting ready for a party. Is there something I can help you with?"

Samantha and Nellie perched awkwardly on the edge of a gold velvet settee, while Eloise sat in the chair opposite them. Feeling a little silly, Samantha told her about the rat. "Our housekeeper is putting out rat traps," she concluded. "But we thought you might want to know about it."

Eloise's smile had vanished. "I don't believe it," she said angrily.

"But our cook, Mrs. Calloway, saw the rat," Samantha persisted.

"Oh, I believe she saw it," Eloise explained.

"But I don't believe a rat just wandered in by itself. This is a new building, and my father makes sure it stays clean and free of pests. The manager even keeps a cat in the cellar to guard against rats and mice."

"But maybe just one or two rats got in," Samantha suggested.

Eloise shook her head so hard that her earrings swung. "No, I think someone caught rats and deliberately brought them into this building."

"Why would anyone do such a thing?" asked Samantha.

"Someone wants to ruin my father," Eloise declared. "Too many things have been happening—like that '13' we saw painted in red. We've had problems with the heat, the electricity has gone off, a water pipe burst— all sorts of 'accidents.' We've actually had residents leave Ravenscourt because they're afraid the building is unlucky." Eloise paused and looked at the girls closely. "Have you heard of the so-called curse?"

Samantha and Nellie exchanged a glance. Then both girls nodded.

"Well, of course you have," Eloise said bitterly. "It seems everyone is talking about it. People are saying my father was cursed by one of his tenants, some silly old lady. It's all complete nonsense, of course. My father takes good care of his properties—even though his tenants are often lazy and undeserving."

Samantha saw Nellie's cheeks flush with anger. "Excuse me, miss," Nellie spoke up. "It's not all nonsense. And the people who live in those buildings do the best they can, but Mr. Raven is a hard landlord."

It was Eloise's turn to go red. "How dare you speak about my father like that!"

Nellie stood her ground. "I once lived across from one of your father's buildings," she said. She gestured at the parlor. "Whole families lived in rooms smaller than this. There were *always* rats in that building. And the old lady you talked about was Grandma Kildany. She wasn't silly. She was half-sick with sorrow because her grandbaby had died and nobody cared—your father least of all. All he cared about was his rent."

"That's a lie!" Eloise exclaimed, rising to her feet. "He may be strict with his tenants, but he's a respectable businessman—and a good father." She gestured at the door. "Perhaps you should leave now."

Nellie nodded, but as the girls were walking out the door, she turned back to Eloise. "Mr. Raven may be a good father, miss," she said softly. "But everything I've told you is true. You should see it for yourself."

As they walked down the hall to their apartment, Samantha whispered to Nellie, "You were so brave!"

"I didn't feel brave," Nellie confessed. "But I couldn't stand there and listen to her say those things." She hung her head. "I guess I just got angry."

"You didn't do anything wrong," Samantha assured her. "You told the truth."

Inside the apartment, Mary and Gertrude

were busy setting rat traps in the kitchen. Samantha and Nellie retreated to their bedroom. Each girl sat on her own bed in silence for a few minutes, remembering the unpleasant scene at the Ravens' apartment. Finally, Samantha broke the silence. "In the building where you used to live—were there really rats all the time?"

Nellie nodded. "Yes." She shivered at the memory. "Some of them were so big, they weren't even scared of my neighbors' cats."

"Ugh!" said Samantha, and her stomach turned over.

Nellie looked up at her friend. "I should tell you something. The first night we were here, I knew there were rats in this building, too. I heard them in the walls. Bridget and Jenny heard them, too. That's one of the reasons they were so scared."

And I was sure it was a squirrel! Samantha thought.

"I suppose I should have said something before," Nellie admitted. "I didn't want to worry anybody."

Samantha wished she could tell Nellie her own secret: that she suspected Aunt Cornelia had gone away because of some "great danger" at Ravenscourt. Yet she couldn't bring herself to say anything that might seem disloyal to Aunt Cornelia. Instead she said, "That's all right, Nellie. I know how you feel."

A knock sounded at the bedroom door. "Samantha, Nellie," Gertrude called. "Miss Raven is here to see you."

What's wrong now? Samantha thought. She and Nellie hurried to the parlor. There they found Eloise standing in front of the fireplace, fidgeting with the strands of pearls around her neck.

"I've been thinking about what you told me," Eloise said, speaking quickly, as if she was in a rush to get the words out. "If it's true, I want to see it for myself. Tomorrow is Saturday. Would you show me the building that you say belongs to my father?"

"It's in a bad neighborhood," Nellie warned. "You wouldn't be safe there."

"Nevertheless, I want to see it," Eloise persisted. "If you don't want to take me there, draw me a map and I'll find it on my own."

Samantha glanced at Nellie, and she saw her friend hesitate.

"I'll take you," Nellie said finally. "And if Grandma Kildany is still there, you can meet her for yourself. But—"she looked at Eloise's pearls and elegant dress—"you shouldn't wear fancy clothes, or jewels either."

"I'll wear something simple," Eloise promised. She turned as if to leave. "I'll call for you tomorrow after lunch."

Samantha took a deep breath and said, "I'd like to go, too." Eloise raised her eyebrows slightly, and Samantha added hurriedly, "Gertrude—she's our housekeeper—would think it odd if Nellie went without me."

Eloise nodded briskly. "Very well, I'll call for you both tomorrow. You can tell your housekeeper that we're going shopping."

After Eloise left, Nellie turned to Samantha. "You don't have to come with us."

A Dangerous Journey

"I *want* to go," Samantha insisted. "We need to find out all the clues we can. Maybe Grandma Kildany will tell us about the curse."

"It could be dangerous," Nellie cautioned. "There are some bad people in that neighborhood."

"If you were brave enough to live there, I guess I can visit," Samantha said loyally. Yet she wondered, *What will we discover?*

7

Clues from the Past

The next morning, Samantha was sitting on her bed brushing her hair when Gertrude called, "Samantha, come quickly! Your aunt is on the telephone."

Samantha dropped her brush and ran down the hall. By the time she reached the telephone, the other girls were already standing there. Nellie was fully dressed, but Bridget, who was now sprinkled all over with chicken pox, was wearing a nightgown and slippers. Jenny had fewer chicken pox than Bridget, but she looked pale. Mary had wrapped her in a blanket and held her tightly in her arms.

"You go first, Jenny," said Gertrude, handing her the earpiece.

Jenny looked at the silver, funnel-shaped

object as if she wasn't sure what to do with it.

"Say hello," Mary urged.

"Hello?" said Jenny, trying to talk into the earpiece.

Mary held the earpiece to Jenny's ear and brought the receiver close to her mouth. "Say hello again. Louder," Mary whispered.

"Hello?" Jenny tried. A look of surprise crossed her face as Aunt Cornelia's voice spoke to her from inside the silver earpiece. There was a very long pause.

"Talk to your aunt," Mary urged. Finally Jenny said softly, "Yes." After another pause, she added, "Yes, she's here." With a look of relief, Jenny handed the silver earpiece to Bridget.

Bridget shifted nervously on her feet as she held the earpiece tight against her ear. "Better, thank you," she told Cornelia. Then she looked down at her arm. "Actually, I have more spots now," she reported. Then she added, "I think so," and "Yes, we are." Finally, she said shyly, "I hope you come home soon."

Next it was Nellie's turn. She answered Aunt Cornelia's questions with a formal politeness that surprised Samantha.

"Yes, ma'am, they are feeling better," Nellie said. "Yes, ma'am, I will," she added. She said good-bye and then handed the earpiece to Samantha.

"I miss you all," Aunt Cornelia told Samantha. Her voice sounded sad and far away.

Why did you leave us? Samantha ached to know. "We miss you, too," she said. She wanted to say more, but Gertrude bustled up and stood with her hands on her hips, waiting impatiently for the earpiece. Samantha turned the telephone over to her.

"Don't you worry about a thing, ma'am. We're all fine here," Gertrude loudly assured Aunt Cornelia.

"When is she coming back?" Bridget whispered to Samantha.

Samantha sighed. "Soon, I hope." Then she smiled at Bridget. "Let's go read a story."

Samantha and Nellie spent the next hour

reading books with the younger girls. Mary came in with a pot of hot chocolate and a platter of dainty buttered rolls.

"Gertrude's saying you must keep up your strength," the maid told Bridget and Jenny firmly. She winked at Samantha and Nellie. "And there's plenty for you, too."

At first, Samantha felt too worried to be hungry. She kept wondering why Aunt Cornelia had left—and what great danger she had been afraid of. And she felt nervous about the upcoming trip with Eloise. Would the tenement be as awful as the place where Nellie had lived with her Uncle Mike? Samantha had once visited that building, and it had taken all her courage just to walk inside and look for Nellie. *At least Nellie will be with me this time,* she thought.

As the other girls sipped hot chocolate and snacked on rolls, Mary made up stories about how Bridget's teddy bear, Fred, was in love with Jenny's doll, Louisa-Jane. Mary's bright, musical laughter was so contagious that Samantha almost forgot her fears. Soon Samantha was laughing with the other girls as Fred chased Louisa-Jane around the room, begging her to marry him.

Later in the morning, while the younger girls rested, Samantha looked through her closet for the right clothes to wear. She pulled out three different dresses for Nellie's approval, but Nellie shook her head at each one. "No, too fancy. We don't want everyone to stare at us." Finally, Samantha, following Nellie's advice, put on a plain, dark blue school dress and pulled her hair back with her oldest ribbon. Nellie wore a similar dress and her plainest hair ribbon.

When it was time for lunch, Nellie and Samantha ate with Bridget and Jenny in the younger girls' room. Just as Mary was carrying away the big silver tray of food, the doorbell rang. Samantha felt her stomach muscles tighten.

Gertrude came down the hall to tell them that Miss Raven had arrived. The housekeeper took one look at Samantha's and Nellie's dresses and declared, "You're not wearing those clothes!" She sounded horrified. "Why, my heavens, you'll look like ragamuffins next to Miss Raven!"

That's how we want to look, Samantha thought. "There's no time for us to change now," she told Gertrude as she and Nellie hurried down the hall.

"Well, keep your coats on!" Gertrude called after them.

The girls met Eloise in the parlor. Samantha was pleased to see that Eloise had dressed in a simple black coat with a matching black-feathered hat, and she seemed in good spirits. As they walked to the elevator, Eloise told Nellie, "I'm sure that there's just been a misunderstanding of some sort. I'm confident this trip will clear it up."

Nellie looked down at the floor but said nothing. When they reached the lobby, the doorman, Martin, was nowhere to be seen. Instead another, older doorman with a bushy black mustache handed them into a horse-drawn cab. "To Macy's in Herald Square," Eloise told the driver.

Samantha and Nellie looked at Eloise with surprise, and she smiled. "I told your house-keeper I was taking you shopping. We'll each get a piece of candy at Macy's."

The driver snapped his reins, and the horses started south. When they reached the towering department store on 34th Street, Eloise told the carriage driver to wait. Inside the bustling store, Eloise expertly threaded through the aisles, and Samantha and Nellie followed her. After they reached the candy counter, Eloise asked, "What would you like?"

After some hesitation, Samantha selected a peppermint stick, Nellie chose a lemon stick, and Eloise picked out a small bag of licorice. Eloise paid for the candy, and they quickly returned to the horse-drawn cab. "Now," Eloise asked Nellie, "how do we find this building that you say belongs to my father?"

"I'm not sure how to find it from here,"

Nellie confessed. "But if you can take us to Union Square, I can show you the way from there."

"Union Square," Eloise told the driver.

Once they reached the square, Nellie directed the driver through narrow streets choked with people and pushcarts. Men with rolled-up shirtsleeves pushed heavy loads, often yelling out in foreign languages. Women carried bags slung over their shoulders, and ragged children darted through the crowds. The cab could hardly move through all the traffic.

Finally, Nellie spotted the street. "There it is," she called out, pointing to a tiny shop on the next block. "I remember the greengrocer on the corner."

Ahead, Samantha saw five-story buildings crammed along both sides of the street. The grimy buildings blocked out the sky and left little light for the crowded sidewalks below. The air was thick with coal smoke and the smell of sewage.

"I can't drive down there, ma'am," the

driver told Eloise. "There ain't room for the horses. Besides, that ain't a place for ladies to go."

He's right, Samantha thought nervously. She saw that Nellie looked worried too, but Eloise seemed more determined than ever.

"We'll stop here," Eloise told the driver. She paid him, and Samantha and Nellie followed her out of the carriage. Cabs were rare in this part of the city, and even though Eloise was dressed simply, she carried with her an unmistakable air of wealth and comfort. A bearded man shambled over to her, his hand held out. "Help the poor, miss? Just a nickel?" Eloise hurried past him.

Nellie led the way to a brown, weary-looking building halfway down the street. Despite the cold weather, two old men were sitting on the front stoop, scarves wrapped around their necks and their hands thrust deeply into the pockets of their worn jackets. The men looked at the girls, and one man said something in a foreign language. They both laughed harshly.

They're laughing at us, Samantha thought nervously.

Nellie climbed the stairs to the building's front door, and Eloise and Samantha followed her. A carved raven hung above the entrance. It looked old and its black paint was chipped, but it was done in the same style as the birds at Ravenscourt. Samantha glanced back at Eloise and saw that she had seen the bird, too.

The building's foyer was a tiny space, about the size of a closet. The floor tiles might once have been pretty, but they were now broken and filthy. Nellie led the way down a hall so narrow that two people could not walk side by side. She knocked at the door of the first apartment, 1A.

A pregnant young woman answered the door. She was carrying a toddler with a smudged face and a tangle of brown curls. The woman's own curly brown hair was pulled back into a braid that straggled past her waist. She looked tired, but she had lively blue eyes. Samantha thought that the woman seemed familiar somehow. *Where have I seen her before?* she wondered.

"Hello," Nellie greeted the woman. "Could you tell me if the Kildany family still lives upstairs?"

The woman gave Nellie an appraising look. "Why are you wantin' to know?"

"We'd like to talk to them," said Eloise, who was standing behind Nellie.

The woman examined Eloise for a moment. "You look all right," she said finally. "So I'll tell ya, they're in 5C, like they've been for years now."

"Is Grandma Kildany . . ." Nellie began.

The woman crossed herself. "Gone to her maker last winter, may she rest in peace."

Samantha felt a wave of relief. She had been dreading meeting the old woman who had cursed Mr. Raven.

"The rest o' the family's there, though," the woman continued, still looking at them curiously.

"Thank you," said Nellie.

Samantha followed Nellie and Eloise up rickety stairs to 5C. There were no windows in the stairway, and it was so dark that Samantha nearly tripped over a man who was curled up on the third-floor landing. He groaned in his sleep but didn't wake as she stumbled over him.

Samantha hurried on. The stairway smelled of urine and unwashed bodies, and she tried to breathe as little as possible. When they finally reached the fifth floor, Nellie knocked at the door of 5C. A skinny, dark-haired girl about Bridget's age opened it a crack and peeked out.

"Do the Kildanys live here?" Nellie asked.

The girl nodded and wiped her nose on the back of her sleeve. Eloise stepped forward and asked the girl who the landlord was. The child looked surprised. "Mr. Raven, o' course."

"May we come in, please?" Eloise phrased it as a question, but it sounded more like an order. Before the girl could say no, Eloise had brushed past her and marched into the apartment. Nellie followed behind her.

Samantha squeezed in last. She found herself

in a small room that smelled of overcooked cabbage and looked as if it served as parlor, kitchen, and dining room all combined. There was a coal stove on the opposite side of the room, but Samantha was sure it didn't have a fire in it. The room was as cold as the windy street outside. In front of the stove sat a rough table with three mismatched chairs.

"May I speak to your parents, please?" Eloise asked the girl. "Or your older brother or sister?"

"Mum and Dad are at the factory. Eileen and Kate too," the girl said, wiping her nose again. "I gotta stay here and watch me sister."

Samantha looked around the apartment to see where the girl's sister might be. Off the kitchen there were two more tiny rooms, each about the size of a pantry. One of the rooms was windowless. All Samantha could see through its open door was the outline of a narrow bed. The other room was slightly larger and had two windows that looked out onto the street. In this room there were mattresses piled with blankets.

The blankets on one of the mattresses moved, and Samantha saw a child about three years old. The little girl scratched her short brown hair and gazed curiously at the visitors.

"Is your sister sick?" Eloise asked. "Is that why she's in bed?"

"Nah, Jenny just stays in there 'cause it's warmer. She gets cold easy, not like me," the older sister said with a hint of pride.

Jenny! Samantha thought with a stab of sorrow. *This is what our Jenny's life could have been like.*

Little Jenny heard her sister say her name. She scrambled out from under the blankets and toddled into the kitchen. Hiding behind her sister's skirts, she peeked out at their visitors.

"Hello," Samantha said softly. She was standing closest to the child and she crouched down so she could look the little girl in the eye. As she did so, she felt the stick of peppermint candy in her pocket. "Would you like this?" she asked, holding it out for the little girl.

With lightning speed, the child snatched the candy and stuck it in her mouth. An angelic smile spread across her face as she tasted the sweet peppermint. Samantha was smiling too as she stood up. Then she happened to glance at the child's head. Her scalp was covered in sores, and there were lice the size of sesame seeds crawling through her hair.

Without even meaning to, Samantha took a step backward. She almost bumped into Nellie, who was standing silently near the door. Samantha felt immediately embarrassed by her reaction, but neither of the Kildany girls had noticed it. Jenny had hidden behind her sister's skirts again. The older girl was answering Eloise's questions.

"It's cold in here," said Eloise, gesturing at the stove. "Why don't you light a fire?"

The child looked as if she'd never heard such a silly question. "All the coal's gone. We've no money for more."

"And what about your rent? Do you always have money for that?" Eloise inquired sharply.

"'Course we do!" the girl said defensively. "If we didn't, Mr. Raven would throw us out, wouldn't he?"

"I see," said Eloise, and patches of color appeared on her cheeks.

Does Eloise think this girl is lying, too? Samantha wondered.

Eloise turned and walked toward the door. Then she stopped, pulled out her purse, and turned back to the girl.

"Here," she said, handing the girl a fistful of money. "Take this and buy food and coal."

The little girl stared at the coins, speechless, while Eloise hurried out of the apartment. Samantha and Nellie followed her down the dark stairs. When they reached the first floor, the pregnant woman was talking in the hall with a boy who held an armful of newspapers. The newspaper boy said something, and the pregnant woman threw back her head and laughed a bright, musical laugh.

As soon as they reached the outside stoop, Samantha took a deep breath. Even the air on the sooty, garbage-filled street smelled clean compared to the foul-smelling tenement building. As she stood on the stoop, Samantha heard the pregnant woman laugh again. Suddenly, she realized why the woman looked so familiar.

8
A FAMILIAR FACE

"Would you wait here a minute, please?" Samantha asked Nellie and Eloise. She stepped back into the building. "Excuse me," she said to the woman, who was still standing in the hallway, chatting. "Do you by chance know Mary Crosby?"

The woman smiled, showing a wide gap in her front teeth. "Well, I should say so! She's me own cousin. We was as alike as twins before I had me babies. She lived right upstairs. She's gone now." The woman paused and looked at Samantha probingly. "Were you wantin' to visit her, too?"

"No," said Samantha. "Thank you anyway." She hurried back outside to Eloise and Nellie.

"I think we've seen enough," said Eloise,

and she began striding quickly down the crowded street. Her mouth was set in an angry line, and she hardly seemed to notice that Samantha and Nellie were struggling to keep up with her.

Once, the girls thought they had lost Eloise in the crowd, but Nellie looked up and saw the black feather on Eloise's hat bobbing in the distance. She pointed out the feather to Samantha. Linking hands, they dodged through waves of people until they caught up with Eloise.

"We almost lost sight of you," Samantha told Eloise breathlessly.

"I'm sorry," Eloise said, slowing down. "I—I was thinking about things." She glanced at the street signs. They had almost reached 14th Street. "We have to take the subway. I gave most of my money away."

Samantha and Nellie followed Eloise down three long flights of stairs, into a cavernous station where the walls were lined with bright mosaics. The air felt damp down here, but it wasn't as cold as the street had been. Eloise paid their nickel subway fares. As they waited on the subway platform for the train that would take them uptown, Samantha looked anxiously into the tunnel. She had ridden on the subway only once before—when it had first been built two years ago. Uncle Gard had been with her then. He had carefully shown her how to get on and off the loud train, and he'd known exactly where to go. *I wish Uncle Gard were here now,* she thought. *He'd know what to do about the Ravenscourt curse.*

It wasn't long before a subway train roared through the tunnel and screeched to a stop in front of them. They climbed aboard. Samantha sat next to Nellie, while Eloise, who still seemed lost in her own thoughts, found a seat across the aisle. The train rumbled through the tunnels until it stopped at 18th Street, not too far from Uncle Gard and Aunt Cornelia's house on Gramercy Park.

As the train waited at the station for new passengers, Samantha's thoughts returned to the dark halls of the tenement. She wondered what it would be like to live in a place where the stove was cold, even in November, and lice were crawling everywhere—

Suddenly, her thoughts were interrupted by a gasp from Nellie. "Is that Aunt Cornelia?"

Samantha looked up sharply. She followed Nellie's gaze to a tall, slim woman who was emerging from the other side of the station. The woman's head was bent so that her hat brim half-covered her face, but she was wearing a familiar fur-trimmed blue coat and carrying a black umbrella with a mahogany handle. Samantha and Nellie leaned close to the window, and they saw the woman turn slightly. There could be no doubt—it *was* Aunt Cornelia. The girls watched her walk briskly toward the station's exit and disappear into the crowd.

As their train pulled away from the station, Nellie whispered, "I thought she was going to her mother's house in Connecticut. Why is she here?"

"I don't know," Samantha admitted as their train entered another dark tunnel. "But we need to find out."

⁊

"Goodness, girls—you look done in!" exclaimed Gertrude when Samantha and Nellie finally returned to the apartment. "Where on earth did you go shopping?"

Samantha and Nellie stole glances at each other. Then they answered in unison, "Macy's."

"Ah," said Gertrude, nodding sagely. "That explains it. Those big stores are enough to wear anyone out. Well, wash up and change. Your tea will be ready soon."

As Samantha sat down for tea, she looked at the dining-room table. It was covered with a white damask cloth and set with shining silverware. She remembered the bare table in the Kildanys' kitchen. *We have so much,* she thought sadly. *And they have so little.*

Thoughts of the tenement and questions about Aunt Cornelia hung over Samantha like a gray fog. At tea, however, she tried to act cheerful for Bridget and Jenny's sakes. The younger girls still were covered in red, itchy spots, but their fevers were gone, and they were feeling well enough to join Samantha and Nellie in the dining room.

"Gertrude had Cook make up gingerbread," Mary informed them as she served them slices from a silver platter. "She thought it'd tempt the little ones' appetites."

Between bites of gingerbread, Bridget and Jenny told about their afternoon's activities. Mary had helped them make puppets in their room and, as a special treat, had let them ride in the service elevator with her when she carried some boxes to the cellar.

"I thought you weren't supposed to leave the apartment," Nellie chided. "What if you give someone chicken pox?"

"Mary said not many people take that elevator, and we didn't meet anyone, either," Bridget said, defending herself.

"It's very big and dark in the cellar," Jenny

reported proudly. "And there are lots of boxes!"

As she watched Jenny enjoy another slice of warm gingerbread, Samantha remembered the other Jenny in the tenement. *I hope she has enough to eat tonight, too,* she thought.

After tea, Mary told Bridget and Jenny that it was time to rest. "If you're quiet as mice for an hour, we'll play puppets later," she promised as she led the younger girls to their room.

Samantha and Nellie escaped to their own room so they could talk in private. As soon as their door was closed, Nellie looked at Samantha questioningly. "Why didn't Aunt Cornelia tell us she was coming home from Connecticut today? And why hasn't she come back to the apartment?"

"I don't know," said Samantha slowly. "I think she might be afraid of something here. I'm not even sure she went to Connecticut at all." Reluctantly, Samantha told Nellie about the 'phone conversation she had overheard. "Aunt Cornelia didn't want to go away," Samantha concluded. "Her mother said she *had* to leave."

Nellie paced around the room, and her blue eyes looked very serious. "Aunt Cornelia doesn't get scared easily," she said at last. "If she's afraid of something, it must be terrible. Maybe she heard of the Ravenscourt curse."

"That can't be it," Samantha protested. "If she thinks the building's cursed, she never would have left us here."

Nellie paced across the room several times. Then, with her back toward Samantha, she said, "Maybe Aunt Cornelia is tired of us. Maybe she doesn't want to be around us anymore."

Samantha remembered how tired Aunt Cornelia had seemed recently. She felt her stomach twist inside. Then she shook her head hard.

"No! Aunt Cornelia's not like that. I could have stayed with Grandmary and the Admiral, but Aunt Cornelia and Uncle Gard invited me to come live with them. And they wanted to adopt you and Bridget and Jenny so we'd all be one family."

"What if they've changed their minds?" Nellie turned to face her, and Samantha saw that there were streaks of tears on her cheeks. "Maybe they've decided four daughters are too many."

For a few minutes, Samantha was silent. She remembered how, after the deaths of their parents, Nellie, Bridget, and Jenny had been left in the care of their Uncle Mike. But one day he had deserted them, leaving Nellie to fend for her little sisters all by herself. *She thinks Aunt Cornelia and Uncle Gard might do that, too,* Samantha thought. She looked for words to convince Nellie that this time would be different. Finally, she said, "Aunt Cornelia sometimes gets angry, doesn't she?"

Nellie looked surprised by the question. "Not often. And she doesn't stay angry long."

"No, but sometimes she loses her temper," Samantha persisted. "And sometimes she worries about us too much, doesn't she?"

"Sometimes," Nellie said with a shrug.

"But would Aunt Cornelia or Uncle Gard

ever do anything that was really mean? Would they ever hurt anybody on purpose?"

"No," Nellie admitted. "They're the kindest people I've ever known. That's why—"

"That's why they wouldn't just leave us." Samantha finished the sentence for her. "There has to be some other reason that Aunt Cornelia went away."

"It must be the curse," Nellie decided. "It's making everything go wrong."

"I don't know," said Samantha. "But maybe if we can understand what's going on in this building, we'll understand why Aunt Cornelia left, too. Let's write down what we've found out, like detectives do."

Samantha went to her schoolbooks and pulled out a pencil, a piece of paper, and a large geography book. She sat down on her bed and, using the book as a writing desk, wrote *Clues* at the top of the paper. Then she poised her pencil. "What do we know so far?" she asked Nellie.

Nellie wiped her face with a handkerchief

and sat down beside Samantha. Together, they drew up a list of facts.

1. *A red 13 was painted on the sign.*
2. *Bridget and Jenny got chicken pox.*

("But they're feeling better now," Samantha added.)

3. *The furnace keeps breaking.*
4. *Rats are in the building.*

Nellie studied the list. "It looks to me like this building really is cursed."

"Yes, but wait," Samantha said. She added:

5. *Grandma Kildany has been dead almost a year.*

"Maybe her curse has outlived her," Nellie suggested. "Remember how Mary told us all the awful things that've happened to Mr. Raven since the curse?"

"Yes, but we can't believe everything Mary

says," Samantha argued. She told Nellie how she'd discovered that Mary had once lived in the same building as the Kildanys, and that Mary's cousin still lived there. "So why did Mary tell us that she doesn't know that part of town very well?"

"I don't know," said Nellie, puzzled.

"I don't either," Samantha said. "Let's add it to the list, though." She wrote:

6. Mary didn't tell the truth.

"And do you remember how guilty Mary looked when we saw her in the lobby, talking to Martin?" Samantha asked.

"Maybe she thought she'd be scolded for taking time from her work," suggested Nellie.

"Maybe," said Samantha. "But if we're watching Martin, maybe we should watch Mary, too—and anyone else who acts strangely." She put one more entry on the list.

7. We should watch everyone at Ravenscourt.

9

CRASH

The next morning was Sunday, and Samantha was relieved to find that the gloomy weather had finally broken. The apartment was still chilly, but sun shone through the windows.

After breakfast, the doorbell rang. It was Eloise. She was wearing a stylish gray hat and coat, and she had Juno on a leash. "Would you like to go for a walk in Central Park with me?" she asked Samantha and Nellie. "It's a lovely day and Juno needs some exercise."

Gertrude gave permission, so the girls put on their coats and went down to the lobby with Eloise. Martin was on duty, and he opened the wide glass doors for them. "Fine morning for a walk," he observed.

The paths of Central Park were busy with strolling families. Eloise smiled and said good morning to several people, but she frowned as she saw a stout, bearded man approaching.

The man tipped his hat. Eloise greeted him with the smallest nod that courtesy allowed. "Hello, Mr. Enderby."

"I hope everything is going well at your father's building, Miss Raven," Mr. Enderby said with a small smirk. "I've heard some disturbing rumors."

"Everything is fine, thank you," Eloise told him curtly. "Good day."

When they reached a part of the path where no one else was in earshot, Eloise turned to Samantha and Nellie. "I've been doing a great deal of thinking since our trip yesterday," she said. "My father's building was worse than I could have imagined. Tell me, Nellie, if you were the landlord there, what changes would you make?"

Nellie thought for a while. "Well, miss," she said cautiously, "a lot of windows are broken, and nobody ever fixes them. It's not so bad in summer, but in winter the wind comes in something terrible."

"So fix the broken windows?" Eloise said.

"Yes and, um . . ." Nellie lowered her voice. "And the, um, necessary rooms. There aren't many of them for all the people in the building."

"More bathrooms," said Eloise. "Yes, that certainly would be a good idea."

Eloise was listening carefully to Nellie as they returned to Ravenscourt together. Martin was still on duty, and he opened the doors with a sweeping gesture. Juno trotted into the building first, and Eloise, Samantha, and Nellie followed. They were crossing the black-and-white marble floor of the lobby when a thunderous crash shook the building, rattling the chandeliers overhead.

"Good gracious heavens!" screamed a tall, well-dressed woman waiting for an elevator. "What was that?"

"It sounded like an elevator crashed!" her husband exclaimed.

Martin sprinted across the lobby and threw open the door to the stairway. He disappeared down the flight of stairs. Eloise dropped Juno's leash and flew after Martin.

"The elevator!" Samantha exclaimed, and she and Nellie raced through the door after Eloise. They ran down a flight of wooden steps. Then they stopped. The dimly lit cellar smelled of smoke and hot metal. At the far end, there was a fog of dust and debris, and the sound of someone prying open metal.

Samantha and Nellie made their way toward the fog at the back of the cellar. There, a service elevator lay flattened and crumpled. Its fall had carved a small crater into the cellar floor. Mr. Winthrop came running down the back stairs. "Great Scott, is anyone hurt?"

Martin stepped back from the wrecked area. "No," he reported. "The service elevator was empty, thank God."

Shaken, Eloise asked how such an accident could have happened. "I thought these new safety elevators were never supposed to fall!"

CRASH

Mr. Winthrop stepped back from the broken elevator and smoothed his well-groomed mustache. "Well, Miss Raven," he said, "all the elevators in the front of the building are the new safety models—nothing can go wrong with them. But to save money, your father installed some of the old-style elevators back here for the servants and cargo. He got them from a building someone was tearing down." Mr. Winthrop surveyed the smoking elevator. "Apparently, this one gave out."

"That seems to be an understatement," Eloise said icily. She drew a deep breath. "The service elevators must be replaced with proper safety elevators," she told him. "Until then, the staff will use the front elevators—along with everyone else."

"But, Miss Raven," Mr. Winthrop began, "your father—"

"My father is away," Eloise told him. "He asked that I look after things here in his absence. I'm sure he will agree with my decision." Eloise turned and saw Samantha and Nellie standing near the door. "You girls had better go upstairs," she told them. "And would you please take Juno to my apartment? I may be here awhile."

Samantha and Nellie slowly climbed the stairs back to the lobby. Several residents had gathered there, and they were all talking angrily about the accident. Samantha heard one man say, "That's it—we're leaving. Nothing works right around this place. It's downright dangerous."

"It's disgraceful! I don't think I'll ever ride another elevator again!" an elderly woman declared.

Nellie gathered up Juno's leash, and she and Samantha led the dog to the main elevator alcove. One of the elevator cars was open and waiting, but Samantha stopped in front of its threshold. She thought about the crumpled pile of smoking metal on the cellar floor. *This is a safety elevator—not like the one that crashed,* she told herself, but she felt her heart beating fast. *What if this building really is cursed? What if . . .*

She looked over at Nellie, who had already

followed Juno into the elevator. Her friend seemed to read her thoughts. "We could walk up the stairs," Nellie offered.

The small man who operated the elevator smiled sympathetically. "I know it's a bit scary, miss, considering all that's happened, but this elevator is as fine as they make anywhere. Safe as houses, it is. Not like that other one."

Samantha nodded. Swallowing hard, she stepped in beside Nellie. "I'm fine," she said, but she began to breathe easily again only when the elevator safely lurched to a stop on their floor.

The girls delivered Juno to the maid at the Ravens' apartment. When they returned to their own apartment, Gertrude met them in the foyer. "Thank goodness you girls are all right," she exclaimed, wringing her hands nervously. "Come with me."

They followed Gertrude into the kitchen, where Samantha was surprised to see Mary and Mrs. Calloway standing solemnly by the stove. Bridget and Jenny were sitting at the kitchen table. When Samantha and Nellie entered, Bridget looked up guiltily. "We didn't mean to do anything wrong," she said.

"What's happened?" Nellie demanded.

Gertrude explained that, unknown to her, Bridget and Jenny had played in the service elevator that very morning. The girls had enjoyed their previous trip to the cellar so much that they had slipped out of the apartment's service entrance and pretended that they were elevator operators, with Louisa-Jane and Fred as passengers.

"We were only playing," Bridget told Nellie.

"They didn't actually run the elevator," admitted Gertrude. "But Mary found them right inside it."

"I scolded them something fierce!" Mary burst out. "I told them never to go *near* that elevator again unless I was with them."

"Not half an hour later we heard the crash," continued Gertrude in a horrified tone. "To think, my little lambs could have been on that elevator!"

Despite their worries, Nellie and Samantha exchanged an amused glance: grumpy old Gertrude had actually called Bridget and Jenny her "little lambs"!

A few minutes later, though, Gertrude had regained her usual bad humor. "You girls go rest, and keep out of my way," she said, dismissing Bridget and Jenny with a wave of her hand. "I have work to do."

Bridget and Jenny asked Mary to play puppets with them again, but Mary shook her head. "Not now," she said, leading the younger girls to their bedroom. "I've work to do, too."

Once they were alone in their own bedroom, Nellie whispered to Samantha, "Do you think the crash was an accident, or the curse?"

"I don't know," Samantha whispered back. "But we have to add it to our list."

Samantha pulled out the sheet of paper and pencil, which she had hidden under her bed. Both girls sat on the floor in front of the fireplace, where Mary had built a fire.

Samantha wrote:

8. Elevator crashed.

"Remember how Martin was the first person to run to the cellar?" Samantha asked.

Nellie nodded. "He seemed to know right away what the problem was."

Samantha thought for a moment and then added one more item:

9. People are moving out of Ravenscourt because they think it's dangerous here.

"It *is* dangerous here," said Nellie. Her eyes looked more worried than ever and she hugged her knees close to herself. "Bridget and Jenny could have been killed today."

❧

Neither Bridget nor Jenny slept well that night, and Nellie was once again called in to reassure Jenny. Left alone in the bedroom, Samantha tried to wait up for Nellie, but finally she fell into an uneasy sleep.

Some time later, she woke up abruptly. She checked to see whether Nellie's return had awakened her, but Nellie's bed was still empty. In the darkness, she heard a faint clicking noise. For a moment, Samantha wasn't sure what it was. Then she recognized the sound of the doorknob turning. There was a moon outside, and by its faint light, she could see the door opening ever so slowly.

Nellie? she thought.

But Nellie did not tiptoe in. Instead, Samantha watched in horror as a white hand slowly reached in through the open door.

10
A MIDNIGHT VISIT

Too scared to move, Samantha stared at the pale hand. It reached forward, hovering over the dresser that stood next to the door. A small white object fluttered from the hand. Samantha heard a gentle rustle as it landed on the dresser top, and she guessed it was a piece of paper. Then the door slowly closed again.

For several long moments, Samantha lay very still in bed, hoping desperately that the door would remain closed. It did, and finally she breathed easily again. *What could possibly be on the paper?* she wondered.

Finally, her curiosity outweighed her fear. She got out of bed and switched on the light by the door. By the bright electric lamp, the small square of folded white paper looked fairly ordinary. She unfolded it and read the scrawled message:

Good by. I have chicken poks and Im going home. You shud leave to. Its not safe heer.
                                        Mary

We're the reason Mary caught chicken pox, Samantha thought as she set the note down on her bedside table. *We have to help her.*

In a moment, Samantha had made up her mind. She slid into her bathrobe and slippers. Then, leaving the bedroom door open, she crossed the hall to the narrow passage that led to the servants' rooms. A light was on in this passage in case the servants had to answer a bell in the middle of the night. Samantha remembered that the first bedroom belonged to Mary. Feeling out of place, she knocked gently on Mary's door. It swung open. The bed was neatly made, but the dresser was bare. Mary was gone.

Returning to the main hall, Samantha

checked the door to the service entrance at the back of the apartment. Gertrude always locked the doors before bedtime, but this door was now unlocked. Samantha felt sure that Mary must have left that way. *If I can just catch up with her, maybe I can convince her to stay.*

Samantha quietly opened the door and slipped out into the service entrance. It was a small space with whitewashed walls and a painted wood floor. By the light of a bulb hanging from the ceiling, Samantha saw that there had been two service elevators here, but both shafts were now boarded up. The signs across them read *CLOSED.*

Across from the elevators, a wooden staircase led to the lower floors. As Samantha started down the stairs, she felt the cold, rough wood through her thin slippers. For a moment, she considered going back to the apartment for her shoes, but then she decided that it would take too much time. *I'll be back in bed soon,* she told herself.

Each landing was lit by a single weak bulb

that cast shadows on the stairs. When Samantha had gone down several flights, she thought she heard a door close far below. She wanted to call out for Mary, but she was afraid of waking other people in the building. She continued down the stairs as quickly as she could.

When she finally arrived on the ground floor, she saw that she was standing in an entryway with two doors. The heavier door seemed to exit to the alley behind the apartment building. It was bolted from the inside. *Mary couldn't have gone out that way,* Samantha reasoned.

Cautiously, Samantha opened the other door and found herself standing at the top of the cellar stairs. She hesitated. It was dark down there, and the air still smelled of overheated metal. The furnace boilers were chugging loudly. Samantha's palms started to sweat. "Mary?" she called out quietly. There was no response.

Mary must be nearby, Samantha told herself. She gathered her courage and started down, gripping the banister tightly. There was no light at the top of these stairs, and the cellar was so dark that Samantha couldn't see when she had reached the final step. But suddenly, the banister ended. She carefully edged her toes forward and found that she was standing on the stone cellar floor.

A bulb was burning somewhere in the cellar. By its dim light, Samantha could see the crushed remains of the service elevator and the crater it had left in the cellar floor. Samantha recalled the horror of that crash. She remembered Mary's scrawled warning: "Its not safe heer."

"Mary?" Samantha called out softly once more. The clunking furnace boilers and the banging pipes drowned out her voice.

Samantha was scared and tired, and her feet were cold. *I'd better leave,* she decided. She was turning to go back upstairs when she heard a man's voice rise above the clattering machines. "You can't leave, not now!"

Samantha's first thought was that the man was talking to her. She froze and listened intently. His voice seemed to come from somewhere in the center of the cellar, halfway between the stairs that led to the lobby and the back service entrance near her.

"I can and I will," Samantha heard Mary say. Her voice was loud and she sounded angry. "I'll not be helpin' you no more."

The man rumbled an answer. Samantha couldn't distinguish all his words, but she heard him say, "...always *some* slight risk involved but..."

Samantha thought the man's voice sounded familiar. *Could it be Mr. Winthrop?* she wondered. Then she realized that the speaker did not have a British accent. *Is it Martin?* She wished she could steal a glance at the man, but she was too afraid of being seen herself. She stepped into the deep shadows near the elevator shaft.

"You're going too far with this curse stuff," Mary told the man. "The broken boilers, the '13,' the rats you brought in—those things didn't hurt nobody. But them two little girls upstairs could've been killed in that elevator. I'd never have forgiven myself. And your money'll do me no good if I end up roasting in hell for my sins."

Listening in the darkness, Samantha realized that this man in the cellar must have deliberately crashed the elevator. *What else is he planning to do?* she wondered. Her mouth felt dry.

"I'm not gonna let ya—" the man began, but then more machines clanged. Samantha couldn't hear the rest of his reply.

When the machines quieted, Samantha heard Mary protesting. "... and I'll not be telling nobody. Raven treated us like dirt when we lived in that hole he calls a building. But I don't want no more of this curse. Someone's gonna get hurt."

A moment later, Mary swished by, her long skirt coming within inches of Samantha's hiding place. Samantha held her breath, hoping that Mary wouldn't notice her standing in the shadows. She heard Mary's shoes click on the wooden steps that led to the service entrance. Then the door at the top of the stairs closed with a bang. Now Samantha knew that she was alone in the cellar with the mysterious man.

Where is he? What is he doing? Samantha tried to listen for sounds of his movements, but the machines began their loud clunking again.

Suddenly, the dim light in the center of the cellar vanished. Samantha blinked her eyes, and then blinked again. By leaning out slightly from her hiding place, she could see a tiny light. It seemed to be moving about. *He must have a pocket torch! What if he comes over here and shines it at me?* She pulled her head back in and crouched down in the shadows.

Then she gasped. Just a few feet away, a pair of glowing eyes were staring at her. She froze, too scared even to scream. The cellar went quiet and Samantha heard a soft mew as the eyes turned away from her. *The manager's cat!* she realized with a rush of relief.

For several long minutes, Samantha waited in the shadows, hoping for a chance to escape. Then the machines rested again. In the quiet, she heard a clank of metal, and then footsteps.

She held herself rigid, but the man didn't pass near her hiding place. Instead he seemed to be walking away in the opposite direction—toward the stairs that led to the lobby. The glimmer of the pocket torch disappeared, and the cellar was blacker than a deep cave.

I have to get out of here, Samantha thought desperately.

She started to inch her way to the back staircase. It was only a few feet away, but she had to be careful to avoid the elevator shaft. She was reaching out her hands to see if she could feel the banister when she heard heavy footsteps coming down the front staircase.

Very carefully, Samantha turned her head. Again she saw a glimmer of light from what she guessed was a pocket torch. She heard another clank of metal and a man's voice declaring, "What the..." She tried to listen hard to what he was saying, but the furnace boilers began to rumble again.

"Martin!" another voice called out loudly

above the noise of the boilers. "What are you doing down there?"

Martin! thought Samantha. *It must be him!*

"Checking the electrical wires, Mr. Winthrop," Martin called back. "The lights went out in the lobby a few minutes ago."

"Don't touch anything!" Mr. Winthrop ordered. "I'll call an electrician in the morning."

"I think I can fix it, sir," Martin shouted.

A few moments later, the single bulb was burning once again. By its feeble light, Samantha saw the staircase, just a foot away. She grasped the skirt of her long robe so it wouldn't rustle. Then she began to tiptoe up the stairs.

At any moment she expected a hand to grab her or a voice to call out, "Stop!" But the stairs were hidden in darkness and the clanking boilers covered the sounds of her steps. When she reached the top of the cellar stairs, she escaped out the door. Then she raced up the service stairs as if a pack of angry dogs were chasing her.

She ran until her legs were quivering and the stabbing pain in her side was so sharp that she couldn't take another step. She stopped and listened for the sound of someone coming after her. Except for the sound of her own gasping, everything was quiet.

As soon as she caught her breath, she kept climbing, taking two steps at a time. Finally, she arrived on the top floor. Panting, she let herself back into the apartment through the service door, locking it behind her. She stopped and breathed deeply. Then she hurried down the silent hall toward her room, where a light still shone through the open doorway. She closed the door behind herself and dove under the covers of her bed.

She was huddled in bed when she heard footsteps in the hall. For one awful second she thought, *He's come after me!* Then Nellie walked into the room.

"I heard you walking around, and then I saw the light on in here," Nellie said with a yawn. "I guess I fell asleep in Bridget and

Jenny's room, and—" She stopped and looked at Samantha more closely. "Something's on your face."

Samantha pulled herself up in bed. There was a hand mirror on her bedside table, and she picked it up and looked at her reflection. Her nose and cheeks were smudged with dust. "I was hiding in the cellar," she began. As she wiped off the dust, she saw that her hand was shaking. She drew her blankets tightly around herself, trying to stop the shaking she felt inside.

"Why were you in the cellar?" Nellie asked, sitting down on the edge of Samantha's bed. "Are you all right?"

Samantha handed her the note that Mary had left them. "It started with this," she said. Then she began to tell Nellie everything that had happened.

Nellie interrupted her halfway through. "You mean it really wasn't the curse that caused the elevator accident—or the other things?"

"Mary said that the man had done them— he'd even brought the rats into the building,"

Samantha told her. "He wanted everyone to believe in the curse."

"What a rotten thing to do!" exclaimed Nellie, her cheeks going red with anger. "He scared all of us. Did you see who it was?"

"No," said Samantha. She explained that she had heard Mr. Winthrop calling to Martin, but she couldn't be sure whether Martin was the same man who had been in the cellar earlier.

When Samantha finished her story, Nellie shook her head sadly. "Oh, Samantha! That must have been awful!"

"The worst part was when it was all dark," Samantha admitted. "I thought I'd never get out."

"Maybe we should talk to Mr. Winthrop and tell him everything you heard," Nellie suggested.

"But all I know for sure is that Mary was talking to a man," Samantha objected. "And if we tell Mr. Winthrop everything, we'll get Mary into trouble. Maybe with the police."

"I wouldn't want that to happen," Nellie said thoughtfully. "Mary seemed so kind. It's hard to believe she tricked us."

"She didn't want to hurt anyone," Samantha pointed out. "And she left us the note to warn us."

"It would have been better if she'd told us the name of the person who is doing all these things," said Nellie.

"She promised the man she wouldn't tell anyone. Maybe they're friends."

"Mary and Martin were friendly," Nellie recalled. "Remember how we saw them talking together in the lobby? And Martin was in the lobby tonight, too."

Samantha nodded. "I know," she said. "That's not enough proof, though."

For several minutes, the girls sat silently. "I wish Aunt Cornelia were here," Samantha said at last. "She'd know what to do."

"But she's not here, and we don't know when she's coming back. And we have to talk to someone," Nellie argued. "We can't wait for more 'accidents.' What if Bridget and Jenny had been on that elevator today?"

Samantha shivered. That possibility was too awful to think about. "If Aunt Cornelia isn't home by the time we get back from school tomorrow, we could talk with Eloise," she suggested.

Nellie considered this idea. "All right," she said at last. "And I'll tell Bridget and Jenny not to set foot out of the apartment tomorrow while we're at school."

Both girls finally got into bed. As Samantha drifted off to sleep, her thoughts returned to the man who had been in the cellar. *What's he going to do next?* she worried.

11
FOOTSTEPS

In the morning, Samantha showed Gertrude the note Mary had left. She explained that she'd found the note on her dresser.

Gertrude glanced at the paper, and then she snorted with disgust. "What a flighty girl!" she exclaimed. "I'll bet she's just making up that bit about chicken pox. She's too lazy to work!"

As Samantha and Nellie left for school, they heard Gertrude grumbling to herself, "And how am I supposed to take care of two sick children and run a household all by myself?"

By the time the girls returned home from school, Gertrude was in an even worse mood. The apartment was cold and Gertrude, who normally prided herself on tidiness, had streaks of coal dust on her white apron. "Keep your coats on—the boilers are out again," Gertrude announced to the girls as she carried coal through the parlor.

"Have you heard from Aunt Cornelia?" Samantha asked hopefully. "Has she said when she'll be home?"

"Soon," Gertrude snapped. "Now don't bother me. Goodness knows, I have enough to do with trying to keep the fires going."

Nellie and Samantha looked at each other. Nellie mouthed, "Eloise?"

Samantha nodded. "We'll be right back," she told the housekeeper, but Gertrude was too busy to notice that the girls were leaving the apartment.

As Nellie knocked at the Ravens' door, Samantha felt a nervous fluttering in her stomach. *What should I say? How can I tell Eloise what happened in the cellar—without getting Mary into trouble?*

The maid came to the door, with Juno yapping at her heels. "I'm sorry, but Miss Raven is out," she said apologetically. "Would you like to leave a message?"

Disappointed, Samantha shook her head. "No, thank you. We'll come back later."

When they returned to their own apartment, the girls looked into Bridget and Jenny's room. The fire in their fireplace was crackling merrily, and dishes from the girls' lunch sat on their bedside table. "We stayed in the apartment, just as you told us," Bridget reported to her sister.

"Gertrude said she didn't want us underfoot, so we kept here in the room 'most all the day," Jenny chimed in. "But see," she said, holding out her arm. "Our poxes are getting better. Do you think we could go outside soon?"

"Do you know when Aunt Cornelia will be coming home?" Bridget asked. "We want to show her our poxes."

"And she'd play games with us, too," Jenny added.

"Oh, I'm sure she'll be home before your chicken pox are gone," said Samantha, trying to sound confident.

"Yes," agreed Nellie. "And we could go outside on the balcony right now. But you'll need to put your coats on."

Samantha helped the younger girls into their warm coats while Nellie opened the drapes and unlocked the French doors that led to the balcony. "There," Nellie said, waving to the open balcony. "It's cold and windy, but you can step out for a moment and get some fresh air."

Bridget and Jenny ventured to the edge of the balcony and leaned against the wrought-iron railing that enclosed it. "Oooh," Jenny exclaimed as the wind blew back her hair. "The lights are just starting to come on."

Samantha walked out and stood beside Jenny. High above the street, the wind brought the scent of the trees in Central Park. Closing her eyes, Samantha breathed deeply. She remembered for a moment the sweet smell of the woods at Piney Point, where she vacationed each summer with Grandmary.

But when she opened her eyes and glanced down, all her happy memories disappeared.

The people and carriages below looked so far away that she felt as if she were teetering on the edge of a cliff. Samantha backed away from the balcony railing and stood in the doorway. There she could safely look out at the buildings outlined against the gray sky.

Standing alone, she watched the other girls peering out delightedly at the street. Then suddenly she heard a noise above her head.

It's probably the wind, she thought at first. She listened harder. There it was again— a low crunching sound, as if someone was walking on the graveled rooftop garden just above their heads.

Samantha reached over and touched Nellie's arm. When Nellie turned, Samantha drew her closer. "Listen," she whispered. "Do you hear something?"

Nellie listened intently. Then she looked at Samantha. "Do you think someone is up there?"

"Maybe," said Samantha, and she heard the crunch of gravel again. "Someone might be out for a walk, I guess."

"It's awfully windy for a walk," Nellie pointed out. She leaned out over the railing and peered up, but the edge of the roof hung over the balcony. "I can't see anything," she said. "Let's go see if someone's there."

Samantha hesitated. Now that they knew that a person—not a curse—was behind the incidents at Ravenscourt, Nellie was determined to find out who that person was. Yet the previous night in the cellar had taught Samantha that she absolutely did not want to follow anyone into a dangerous place—not ever again.

But a detective has *to investigate,* Samantha told herself.

She glanced at the sky. There was still some light left. Surely they would be safe going up on the roof in the daylight. "All right," she told Nellie. "But we'll have to hurry."

Nellie nodded, and then she called to Bridget and Jenny. "Let's go inside. I don't want you to get chilled. Besides, tea will be ready soon."

While Bridget and Jenny tidied themselves

for afternoon tea, Samantha and Nellie headed for the front door. They had almost reached it when Gertrude's sharp voice stopped them. "Where do you girls think you're going?"

Samantha and Nellie shared a guilty glance. Then Samantha turned a bright smile on the housekeeper. "We're just going up to the roof garden for a few minutes. It's awfully stuffy in here."

Gertrude looked at them as if they came from some strange species. "Stuffy! It's all I can do to keep warm!" she exclaimed. Then she sighed, "Well, I suppose you may go up for a few minutes, but don't go near the edge. We've enough problems without one of you falling off the building. And be back soon. Your tea will be ready shortly—and Cook's made hot chocolate, too."

Samantha and Nellie hurried out to the elevator alcove, opened the door to the stairs, and climbed up. The door at the top of the stairs was closed. Samantha half hoped it would be locked and they could go back downstairs and wait for their steaming cups of hot chocolate. But Nellie tried the door and it opened. Samantha watched her friend step out cautiously.

"What do you see?" Samantha whispered.

"Nothing," Nellie whispered back. "The chimney's in the way." She crept out on the roof, and reluctantly Samantha followed.

When they reached the square brick chimney, they crouched behind it. Then they peeked out. At first, Samantha did not see anything out of the ordinary. She breathed a sigh of relief. *Well, we tried,* she thought. *Now we can go back and—*

Suddenly, Nellie grabbed her arm and gestured toward the corner of the roof.

12
THE RAVEN FLIES

Samantha followed Nellie's gaze. On their right, about forty feet from where she and Nellie were hiding, a man was standing near the edge of the roof. His back was to the girls, and he had a large hammer in his hands. He seemed to be working on the huge, carved black raven that was perched on that corner of the wall.

"That must be who we heard," Nellie whispered. "Our balcony's just below him."

"Maybe he's a repairman," Samantha whispered back.

Nellie shook her head. "No. Look at his clothes."

Samantha looked closely at the man. He looked tall and heavyset, and he was wearing a dark suit. He was hatless, and in the fading afternoon light his hair appeared black or dark brown, but definitely not red. *It's not Martin,* Samantha thought. *Who is it—and what's he doing?*

The man turned around and picked up a crowbar. Samantha saw the flash of a gold pocket watch across the man's stomach. Then she glimpsed his face.

"It's Mr. Winthrop," she and Nellie whispered in unison. Samantha realized that the mysterious person walking on the rooftop was actually the building's manager. "He must be fixing something on that statue," she told Nellie.

Both girls stood up from their hiding place. "Let's see what he's doing," Nellie suggested.

Mr. Winthrop had turned back to the raven, so he did not see the girls crossing the rooftop garden. As they approached him, Samantha noted that he seemed to be prying at the raven with the crowbar. The bird was at least six feet across at its wingspan, and it looked heavy.

I hope it doesn't fall, Samantha worried. *I wonder if we should help him.*

The wind was picking up. Samantha was just about to call out to Mr. Winthrop when she saw him push down on the crowbar. The raven teetered for a moment on the edge of the wall. Then it fell headfirst, diving toward the ground.

"Oh, no!" cried Nellie. A moment later, there was a loud crash.

Samantha and Nellie rushed to the wall to see if the falling sculpture had hit anyone on the street. They were relieved to find that the sidewalk was empty. Only the shattered bird lay below them. Peering down at the ground, Samantha once again felt sick to her stomach. She pulled herself back from the wall and looked up at Mr. Winthrop.

His face was white. "Wha—what are you girls doin' here?" he demanded.

"We heard noises on the roof, and we wondered who was up here," Samantha told him. "When we saw it was you, we thought you might need some help." She glanced at the raven's empty perch. "I guess we were too late."

Mr. Winthrop scowled at her. "That raven was loose," he explained. "I was tryin' to tighten it."

Samantha noticed that Mr. Winthrop wasn't talking with a proper English accent anymore. *I wonder if he just pretends to be English because he thinks it will impress people,* she thought.

"I'm glad that statue didn't hit anybody," said Nellie. "Somebody could have been killed."

"Of course there's always *some* slight risk involved when you do repairs such as this," Mr. Winthrop said, regaining his English accent. He drew himself up in a dignified manner. "But there wouldn't have been a problem if you girls hadn't surprised me. You really should be more careful."

We should be more careful! Samantha thought indignantly. *He's the one who dropped the statue. Besides, he didn't even know we were here until after it fell . . .*

Suddenly, suspicion stabbed at Samantha. Mr. Winthrop hadn't really been tightening the statue at all, she realized. He'd been prying it up with the crowbar. And she'd heard the phrase "always *some* slight risk involved" before—that was exactly how the man in the cellar had said it last night!

Terror gripped Samantha as Mr. Winthrop studied her and Nellie.

"Well, I'm sure you girls meant no harm," he said finally, stroking his mustache thoughtfully. "I'm sure you didn't *intend* to startle me, so I won't make a complaint to your parents. If I did make a complaint, your parents would have to pay to replace the statue, and that would be *very* expensive."

Mr. Winthrop smiled down at them. "I wouldn't want you girls to get into trouble, so we'll just tell everyone that a gust of wind blew the raven over. It will be our little secret, won't it?"

"But it wasn't our fault," Nellie protested.

"That's all right," interjected Samantha, her

heart beating wildly. She grabbed Nellie's hand. "We're sorry we bothered you, Mr. Winthrop. We'd better go now."

Nellie turned to her, and her eyes asked silently, *What are you doing?* Samantha looked pointedly at the crowbar, and then at Mr. Winthrop.

Suddenly, Nellie understood. In a voice filled with forced cheerfulness, she told Mr. Winthrop, "Yes, sorry, but we have to go. Our tea is ready." Nellie tugged on Samantha's hand and together they turned and sprinted toward the door. But before they could even reach the chimney, Mr. Winthrop caught up with them.

"Wait!" he called out, grabbing Samantha by the shoulder. He whirled her around to face him, and she lost hold of Nellie's hand.

"You mustn't say anything about this to anyone," Mr. Winthrop ordered. He gripped Samantha's shoulder so tightly that her bones felt pinched even through the thickness of her woolen coat. "You must—"

Nellie had almost reached the door before she realized that Mr. Winthrop was holding Samantha. Nellie turned back. "LET HER GO!" she yelled and kicked Mr. Winthrop in the shin.

"Aaahhh!" he exclaimed, and for a moment he loosened his grip. As Samantha and Nellie turned to run again, he shot forward and grabbed them by the velvet collars of their coats.

The girls kicked and struggled to get free. They threw Mr. Winthrop off balance, and he fell onto one knee. But he still kept hold of their collars.

Samantha felt herself being dragged farther from the door. She dug her feet into the graveled rooftop and struggled against Mr. Winthrop with all her strength.

"NO!" she yelled. "NO!"

13
DETECTIVE WORK

Suddenly, Samantha heard a loud crack.

Mr. Winthrop yelped in pain, and Samantha looked up. She was amazed to see Aunt Cornelia standing over the big man, her heavy umbrella poised above his head.

"Take your hands off my daughters!" Aunt Cornelia commanded, her face white with fury. "Or, by heaven, I'll split your skull."

"I don't think that'll be necessary, Mrs. Edwards," a man's voice declared. Martin suddenly appeared behind Aunt Cornelia. He was breathing hard, as if he'd run up flights of stairs, and he had a gun in his hand.

Samantha stared at the long black barrel of Martin's gun. She froze, terrified that at any second he would turn the gun on her. But the doorman held the gun steady, aiming it straight at Mr. Winthrop.

"Let the girls go, Winthrop," Martin ordered the manager. "And put your hands behind your back."

As soon as Mr. Winthrop released his grip on their collars, Samantha and Nellie pulled themselves off the ground and ran to Aunt Cornelia. "Oh, my dears!" she exclaimed, gathering them in her arms. "Did he hurt you?"

Samantha and Nellie assured her that they were unharmed. Standing close to Aunt Cornelia, they watched as Martin handcuffed Mr. Winthrop and then pulled the startled manager to his feet.

"Martin, this is an outrage!" Mr. Winthrop blustered. "Let me go immediately, or you'll lose your job!"

"I'm afraid not, sir," Martin said calmly. "You see, I'm not really a doorman. I'm a Pinkerton detective, and it's my job now to take you to the police."

Samantha and Nellie stared at each other,

amazed. *A Pinkerton detective!* Samantha thought. *That's why he's always around when there's trouble.*

"No, no, you don't understand," Mr. Winthrop said angrily. "I found these girls up here. They'd pushed that raven off the roof. I was trying to stop them so they wouldn't cause more trouble."

"That's not true!" Nellie exploded.

Aunt Cornelia spoke up loyally. "Of course it's not true," she said, holding Samantha and Nellie close to her. "My girls would never do such a thing!"

"Mr. Winthrop's the one causing the trouble," Samantha declared. "He's the one who's been trying to make us believe that Ravenscourt is cursed."

Together, she and Nellie told how they'd seen the building manager push the raven off the wall. "He knew we'd seen him, and he wanted us to promise we wouldn't tell," Nellie explained.

"But we know he did the other things, too,"

Samantha added. "The elevator crash, the rats, the furnace breaking down, and even the '13' on the sign—I heard him talking to Mary about them. She ran away because she was afraid someone would get hurt."

"You heard all that?" Mr. Winthrop asked incredulously.

Samantha nodded.

Mr. Winthrop looked from Samantha's face to Martin's gun. Suddenly, his blustery dignity deflated like a popped balloon. "All right, I may've played a few tricks," he confessed, his English accent now gone completely. "But I wasn't gonna hurt anyone—I was just gonna scare people into moving outta here. It was Enderby's idea! *He* paid me to do it!"

Martin gestured toward the door. "Why don't you explain all that to the police?" he said, directing Mr. Winthrop down the stairs.

Aunt Cornelia, Nellie, and Samantha followed them at a safe distance. "I'm glad you came when you did," Samantha said, holding tight to Aunt Cornelia's hand.

"So am I," she agreed. "Gertrude told me you were up on the roof garden. I decided to come up and surprise you. When I stepped out and saw that man attacking you . . ." Aunt Cornelia shuddered. "Well, I've never been so angry in my entire life." She stopped halfway down the stairs and hugged the girls again. "I'm so glad you weren't hurt."

When they reached the bottom of the stairs, Martin and Mr. Winthrop were standing by the elevators, waiting for the next available car. An elevator door opened, and a familiar figure stepped out.

"Gardner!" Aunt Cornelia exclaimed.

"Hello!" Uncle Gard greeted them cheerfully. "I finished my business in Boston and came home early. I hope—" He broke off in mid-sentence as his eyes took in Mr. Winthrop, who was standing silently in handcuffs, and Martin, who was guarding the building manager.

"What's going on?" Uncle Gard demanded.

Martin explained that he was a Pinkerton detective, hired by Mr. Raven to investigate all the "accidents" that had been occurring at Ravenscourt. "Mr. Raven suspected that Enderby was behind it all," said Martin. "But he didn't know who Enderby had hired to do his dirty work. I've had my eye on Mr. Winthrop here for a long time—especially since I found a jar of red paint in his office. And then last night, I was almost sure he was the one who had shut off the electricity in the building. But I wasn't able to prove anything against Winthrop till your daughters helped me out."

Uncle Gard raised his eyebrows. "How did they help?"

"Well," said Martin, "I was in front of the building, and one of the ravens came flying off the roof. When I looked up, I saw someone up there, and I guessed it was Winthrop. I probably couldn't have caught him in the act, though, if it hadn't been for these young ladies.

"They're good fighters," Martin added with a grin. "I got up there as fast as I could, but it seems the girls and Mrs. Edwards were taking care of Mr. Winthrop on their own."

"Fighting on the roof?" said Uncle Gard, sounding astonished. He turned to Aunt Cornelia, Samantha, and Nellie. "Are you all right? What's been happening here?"

Aunt Cornelia took his arm. "Let's go inside. We have a lot to talk about."

Inside the apartment, Uncle Gard hugged Bridget and Jenny, and they proudly showed him their chicken pox. The whole family gathered in the parlor, and the girls took turns telling Uncle Gard about the past few days. Neither Samantha nor Nellie, however, mentioned that they had seen Aunt Cornelia in the subway station.

Samantha hoped that Aunt Cornelia would volunteer her reasons for leaving Ravenscourt, but Aunt Cornelia and Uncle Gard just sat together and listened intently to the girls' adventures. When Aunt Cornelia learned about the elevator crash, she put her arms around Bridget and Jenny. "Oh!" she exclaimed, holding them close. "Thank heavens you weren't hurt!"

DETECTIVE WORK

After the girls had finished telling their stories, Uncle Gard shook his head. "Chicken pox, rats, no heat, and an elevator crash—and then an attack on the roof!" He stood up. "Come on, girls, pack up your things. I don't care if our house is still unfinished. We're going home. Tonight."

Samantha and Nellie grinned at each other, and Bridget and Jenny clapped their hands with delight. Aunt Cornelia smiled, too. "Oh, Gard, that *would* be nice."

They were almost finished packing when Eloise knocked at the door. "I saw your trunks in the hall," she said as Gertrude escorted her into the parlor, where the whole family was assembled. "You're leaving, aren't you? Well, I really can't blame you. I'm so sorry for everything that's happened during your stay."

Eloise looked so downcast that even the feather on her hat seemed to be drooping. Aunt Cornelia invited her to take a seat. "It wasn't your fault, Eloise," Aunt Cornelia reassured her. "How were you to know that Mr. Enderby was trying to make life miserable for everyone at Ravenscourt?"

"Well, because of Winthrop's confession, Mr. Enderby's going to be arrested," said Eloise. "He will probably have to pay Father a very large fine for all the damage he's caused us."

"Your father must be angry," Aunt Cornelia sympathized.

"Actually, Father is thrilled to have triumphed over Mr. Enderby," Eloise admitted. "The two of them have been enemies as long as I can remember."

"Was it Mr. Enderby who started everyone talking about the curse again?" Samantha asked.

Eloise nodded. She explained that Mr. Enderby had heard the story of the curse a few years ago. When the workman died during Ravenscourt's construction, Mr. Enderby decided to revive the story. Through a series of planned "accidents," he hoped to convince tenants that Ravenscourt was cursed.

"Father and I had a long talk, and I told

him how I'd visited one of his tenements," Eloise confided. "At first he was angry, but he finally forgave me. I've asked him to use the money he'll get from Mr. Enderby to make his buildings decent places to live. I told him that if he improves his buildings, people will no longer mention the old curse—all they'll talk about is the good he's doing."

Eloise smiled and leaned forward eagerly in her chair. "I've even thought of a new name for the buildings—'Raven's Havens.' Father liked that."

"Do you think he'll really do it?" Aunt Cornelia asked. "It would make such a difference in so many people's lives."

Eloise stuck out her chin, and for a moment she looked just like her father. "I think I'll be able to persuade him," she said. "But I'd appreciate any advice you could offer, Mrs. Edwards."

Aunt Cornelia invited Eloise to come to tea the following week to talk about plans to improve the tenements. "And you can see our renovations, too," she added, her eyes sparkling. "We have some surprises that even the girls don't know about yet."

"What? What?" Bridget, Jenny, Nellie, and Samantha all asked at once.

Uncle Gard laughed. "Finish packing and you'll see."

14

A SURPRISE ANNOUNCEMENT

As they drove home through the twinkling lights of the city, Samantha tried to imagine what Aunt Cornelia had meant by "some surprises." *Will she ever tell us why she left?*

When they walked into the house, Samantha breathed a sigh of relief. Even though it smelled of sawdust and fresh paint, it felt like home. "You probably don't want to see your new rooms, do you, girls?" Uncle Gard teased.

"We do!" they all said at once. Together, they climbed the stairs to the attic. "Youngest first," Uncle Gard declared, and he let Jenny through the door, followed by Bridget, then Samantha and Nellie.

Jenny gasped. Bridget said, "Oooooooh!" "Jiminy!" said Samantha, and Nellie was speechless. The dark old attic had been turned into a bright, cheerful space with a vaulted ceiling and big bay windows. Along one wall was a small library, with built-in bookshelves and cozy chairs. Across from the library was a bathroom and a large play area, with two swings hanging from the attic rafters. Against the longest wall there were three pretty cottages, each about the size of a large tent.

"They're like little houses!" declared Jenny.

"The builders have not quite finished them yet," said Cornelia, smiling. "So you girls can choose the colors you'd like." The first cottage had *Samantha and Nellie* written on a nameplate over the front door. The middle cottage said *Bridget and Jenny.* The nameplate on the third cottage was blank.

The girls explored their new rooms. Each had two beds, two dressers, and two trunks for toys. The walls between the cottages were sliding doors that could be opened when the girls wanted to be together, or closed when they wanted privacy.

Samantha loved the little cottages, but she saw that Nellie was standing alone in the library area, tears trickling down her cheeks. Samantha went over to her. "Are you all right?" she asked.

Nellie nodded, but her tears began streaming harder. Bridget and Jenny clustered around Nellie. The younger girls looked confused; it wasn't like their big sister to be upset.

Uncle Gard and Aunt Cornelia joined them. "Nellie, what's wrong?" Aunt Cornelia asked. "Isn't it what you hoped for?"

Nellie shook her head. "It's all perfect," she said. "But, but—" She began to sob. "I'd been thinking you didn't want us anymore."

"Oh no, dear!" Aunt Cornelia exclaimed, and she reached out and gently stroked Nellie's hair. "Whatever gave you that idea?"

Samantha and Nellie looked at each other. Then Samantha decided it was time to speak. "I'm sorry, Aunt Cornelia, but when your mother called Ravenscourt, I was the one who answered the telephone. At first your mother thought she was speaking to you, and she said you should leave us because you were in danger."

Nellie looked up through her tears. "And on Saturday, we saw you in the subway station. So we knew you weren't really in Connecticut."

"I see," Aunt Cornelia said softly. "Well, I think we should talk." She sat down in one of the cozy armchairs, and Uncle Gard pulled up a chair beside her. The four girls gathered around them.

"I'm so sorry I didn't tell you the truth," Aunt Cornelia began.

"You mustn't be too hard on yourself, Cornelia," Uncle Gard interjected. "You did it for a good reason."

"I did mean well," Aunt Cornelia agreed. "And, oh my dears, you're wrong if you thought I *wanted* to leave—I missed you terribly."

Bridget's gray eyes widened. "But why did you go?"

"Well," said Aunt Cornelia, "when you and Jenny came down with chicken pox, I became worried. I wasn't sure if I'd had it. I 'phoned my mother and she didn't remember either."

"So you thought you might catch chicken pox?" Samantha asked.

"Yes. The doctor told me that although chicken pox is usually not serious in children, it can be very serious in adults. He warned me to stay away until your chicken pox sores had healed." Aunt Cornelia sighed. "I'm sorry I didn't tell you my real reason for leaving, but I didn't want you to worry about me."

"Is there still a chance you could get it?" asked Nellie, concerned.

"No," said Aunt Cornelia. "My mother thought to telegraph my nanny. She's retired now, but she remembered that I'd had chicken pox when I was two. So I knew it was safe to come home."

Jenny, who had wandered away to explore the attic, came back and tugged eagerly on Aunt Cornelia's sleeve. "Who is that house for?" she asked, pointing to the third cottage. "There's one without a name on it."

Aunt Cornelia and Uncle Gard looked at each other. "Well," Uncle Gard began, "other children might come to stay here, too."

"You mean like Agatha and Agnes?" Samantha asked.

"Or Alice?" inquired Jenny.

"Yeessss," Uncle Gard said slowly. "Those are all very nice children. But a little baby might be nice, too."

A baby! The girls turned to look at Aunt Cornelia. She nodded, and her eyes sparkled with joy. "Yes, my dears. We're expecting a baby—probably sometime around Easter."

For a moment, there was a stunned silence. Samantha suddenly guessed why Mrs. Pitt had warned of a "great danger." Hesitantly, she asked Aunt Cornelia, "Were you afraid that if you got chicken pox, it might be bad for the baby?"

"Yes, but there's nothing to worry about now," Aunt Cornelia said reassuringly. She smiled at the girls. "Do you think you'll enjoy having a new baby in the house?"

A SURPRISE ANNOUNCEMENT

Nellie, Bridget, and Jenny all began to talk at once.

"We could play with her!" exclaimed Jenny.

"Could we carry her?" asked Bridget.

"We can help you feed and change her," Nellie offered eagerly.

"A baby sister!" Samantha sighed. "How wonderful!" Then she thought for a moment. "Or I guess it could be a brother, couldn't it? That would be fine too, I suppose."

"We don't know what the baby will be," Uncle Gard said, smiling. "All we know is that we'll never love her—or him—more than the four beautiful daughters we already have."

We're really home, Samantha thought happily, as she and her sisters hugged Uncle Gard and Aunt Cornelia. *Home at last!*

LOOKING BACK

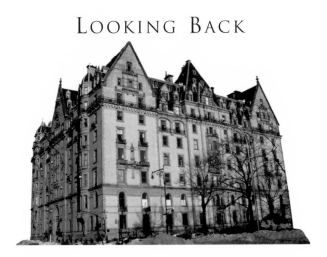

A PEEK INTO THE PAST

A ghostly figure appears before an amazed audience.

In Samantha's time, Americans were swept up in a fascination with mysteries and the supernatural. The Sherlock Holmes stories, with their spine-tingling plots, were bestsellers.

By the end of each story, the great detective always discovers a perfectly normal explanation for the strange events—but the author, Sir Arthur Conan Doyle, really did believe in the existence of spirits who could interact with the living. This belief was shared by many,

The fictional detective Sherlock Holmes and one of his spookiest stories

and unscrupulous businesspeople sometimes took advantage of such beliefs.

About fifty years before Samantha was born, in a small town in New York, two sisters named Kate and Maggie Fox heard loud knockings in the house their family had moved into a few days before. At first the family was terribly frightened, but soon the girls reported that they could talk to whatever was causing the knocking and receive answers in the form of knocks.

Kate and Maggie Fox

Word spread, and hundreds of people began coming to the Foxes' home each night to see Maggie, age 11, and Kate, 14, talk with the spirit. Some people thought the whole thing was faked, but others believed the Fox sisters had special powers. As they grew up, the sisters billed themselves as *mediums*, or spirit-communicators, and they gave eerie nighttime performances for decades. Often people in the audience would ask the sisters to contact the spirits of loved ones who had died.

A nineteenth-century séance

Years later, the sisters confessed to faking their powers, but such performances, called *séances*, continued to be popular throughout the early 1900s, when Samantha was a girl. During the same period, other performers held "ghost shows" in which they thrilled audiences with amazing apparitions—and then showed how

A projectionist (lower right) creates a "ghost" on the stage.

the ghosts had been created with actors and trick lighting, to prove that they were just special effects. These performers believed that most mediums were really frauds preying on a gullible public for money—a bit like Mr. Winthrop in Samantha's story.

In his scheme to frighten people away from Ravenscourt, Mr. Winthrop used a common source of public anxiety—elevators. Early elevators were so dangerous that they were used only to carry freight, not people; that way, if the cable broke, nobody would be killed. By Samantha's time, safety elevators had been developed, with a spring-loaded device to catch the elevator if the cable snapped. But elevators still made many people nervous. It just seemed scary to ride through the air in a box suspended from a cable.

Safety elevators led to the construction of taller

Illustration of a safety elevator surviving a broken cable

These girls operated an elevator at a department store.

buildings, since people no longer had to climb long flights of stairs. In the old-style "walk-ups," upper-story apartments were the cheapest because of all the stairs to climb, but in the new "skyscrapers," the top floors were the most expensive, owing to their dramatic views and distance from the city's dirt and noise. By moving onto the very top floor at Ravenscourt, Samantha's family would have had one of the nicest apartments in the building.

However, taller buildings presented an odd problem for their owners: what to do about the 13th floor. The number 13 was widely held to be unlucky, and owners of hotels and apart-ment buildings

The Dakota, one of New York's first high-rise luxury apartment buildings

knew that many people would refuse rooms on the 13th floor. So they played tricks with the numbering system. If the building had 13 floors, like Ravenscourt, the numbering started on the second floor, and the elevator button for the first floor was labeled "Lobby" or "Ground," as Samantha observed. In taller buildings, the numbering simply skipped 13 and went straight from 12 to 14! This superstition was another common fear that Mr. Winthrop exploited in his scheme.

Today, elevators are part of our everyday lives, and most of us think nothing of them. But superstitions linger. The next time you go into a tall building, check the elevator panel to see if it skips the 13th floor!

Even many modern buildings avoid the "unlucky" number.

AUTHOR'S NOTE

Ravenscourt is fictional, but during Samantha's time, luxurious apartment buildings were becoming popular for wealthy New Yorkers. I learned a lot about these buildings through *Alone Together: A History of New York's Early Apartments* by Elizabeth Collins Cromley and *New York, New York: How the Apartment House Transformed the Life of the City (1869–1930)* by Elizabeth Hawes. The archivist at the Otis Elevator Company referred me to photos of elevators from the turn of the last century.

I'm grateful to the doormen who allowed me to peek inside some of New York's elegant old apartment buildings. I'm also glad to have had the opportunity to visit The Lower East Side Tenement Museum in New York City. Through its guided tours, this museum helps visitors imagine what life was like in an overcrowded tenement.

ABOUT THE AUTHOR

Sarah Masters Buckey grew
up in New Jersey, where her
favorite hobbies were swimming
in the summer, sledding in the
winter, and reading all year round.

She and her family now live in New
Hampshire and enjoy visiting New York City.
She is the author of *Samantha's Special Talent,* as
well as three American Girl History Mysteries:
The Smuggler's Treasure, Enemy in the Fort, and
Gangsters at the Grand Atlantic, which was
nominated for the 2004 Agatha Award for Best
Children's/Young Adult Mystery.